"Secrets and suspense abound on the luxury cruise of the SS *Morro Castle*, as two women, both determined to exact justice, hurtle on an unalterable course toward an uncertain future. *The Cuban Heiress* swept me into the story and held me riveted through the last page."

—Shelley Freydont Noble, *New York Times* bestselling author of *The Tiffany Girls*

"A tense, compelling thriller in which we are never sure who is the hunter and who the hunted."

—Rhys Bowen, *New York Times* bestselling author of *Peril in Paris*

"Based on a shocking and little-known moment from history, Chanel Cleeton has woven a twisting tale of murder, revenge, and romance that I simply could not stop thinking about!"

—Stephanie Marie Thornton, *USA Today* bestselling author of *Her Lost Words*

"A novel of audacious risk and survival that will hold you tight in its grip from first page to last."

—Tessa Arlen, *USA Today* bestselling author of *In Royal Service to the Queen*

"Brimming with romance, intrigue, and danger, this cleverly written tale twists and turns all the way to the final page. I absolutely couldn't put this book down!"

—Kristin Beck, author of *The Winter Orphans*

"I loved *The Cuban Heiress*. It is a compelling novel of two women facing betrayal, intrigue, and murder that captivated me from the start and held me until the emotional end."

—Georgie Blalock, author of *An Indiscreet Princess*

PRAISE FOR THE NOVELS OF CHANEL CLEETON

"A beautiful novel that's full of forbidden passions, family secrets, and a lot of courage and sacrifice."   —Reese Witherspoon

"A sweeping love story and tale of courage and familial and patriotic legacy that spans generations."

—*Entertainment Weekly*

"*Next Year in Havana* reminds us that while love is complicated and occasionally heartbreaking, it's always worth the risk."

—NPR

"A thrilling story about love, loss, and what we will do to go home again. Utterly unputdownable."   —PopSugar

"A remarkable writer."   —*The Washington Post*

"You won't be able to put this one down."   —*Cosmopolitan*

BERKLEY TITLES BY CHANEL CLEETON

Next Year in Havana

When We Left Cuba

The Last Train to Key West

The Most Beautiful Girl in Cuba

Our Last Days in Barcelona

The Cuban Heiress

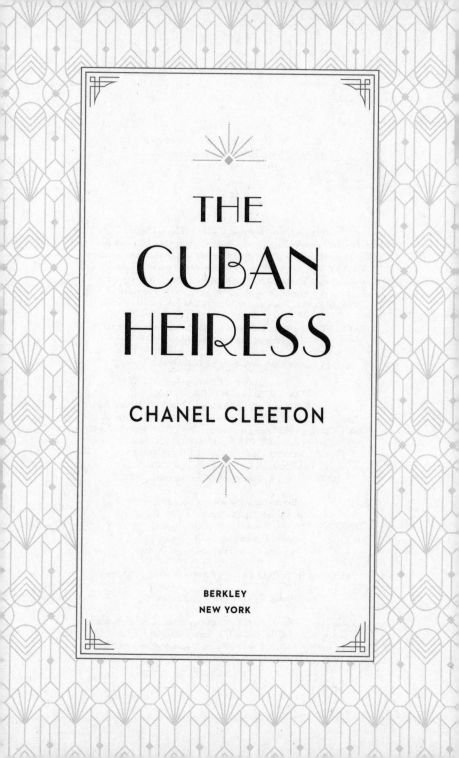

THE
CUBAN
HEIRESS

CHANEL CLEETON

BERKLEY

NEW YORK

BERKLEY
An imprint of Penguin Random House LLC
penguinrandomhouse.com

Ⓟ

Copyright © 2023 by Chanel Cleeton
"Readers Guide" copyright © 2023 by Chanel Cleeton
Penguin Random House supports copyright. Copyright fuels creativity,
encourages diverse voices, promotes free speech, and creates a vibrant culture.
Thank you for buying an authorized edition of this book and for complying
with copyright laws by not reproducing, scanning, or distributing any part
of it in any form without permission. You are supporting writers and allowing
Penguin Random House to continue to publish books for every reader.

BERKLEY is a registered trademark and the B colophon is a trademark of
Penguin Random House LLC.

Library of Congress Cataloging-in-Publication Data

Names: Cleeton, Chanel, author.
Title: The Cuban heiress / Chanel Cleeton.
Description: Berkley trade paperback edition. | New York: Berkley, 2023.
Identifiers: LCCN 2022054126 (print) | LCCN 2022054127 (ebook) |
ISBN 9780593440483 (trade paperback) | ISBN 9780593440490 (ebook)
Classification: LCC PS3603.L455445 C83 2023 (print) |
LCC PS3603.L455445 (ebook) | DDC 813/.6—dc23
LC record available at https://lccn.loc.gov/2022054126
LC ebook record available at https://lccn.loc.gov/2022054127

Berkley hardcover edition / April 2023
Berkley trade paperback edition / April 2023

Printed in the United States of America
1st Printing

Title page art: Art deco pattern © AlevtinaZ / Shutterstock.com

Book design by Kristin del Rosario

THE
CUBAN
HEIRESS

CHAPTER ONE

ELENA

The dead woman stands in the line for the tourist-class passengers, her shoes pinching her toes, the cheap fabric of her dress itching her skin. The *Morro Castle*'s diligent clerk examines her papers—the fake passport, the assumed name Elena Reyes—hopefully flawless enough to pass muster. She certainly paid enough for them, money she could ill afford.

The clerk glances down at Elena's photograph on the documents and back at her face again, comparing the two for any obvious differences.

The photo itself is genuine, the image contained there of a young Cuban woman looking surprisingly vibrant considering she is essentially—for practical purposes, at least—a ghost. It was taken two weeks ago in an apartment building in Greenwich

Village by a man to whom Elena gave nearly her entire life savings to be able to get on this ship.

It was worth every penny and then some.

The clerk waves her on.

A group of women pass by, their laughter spilling out onto the gangway.

Her fellow passengers are in high spirits despite the tourist-class accommodations, their excitement over their weeklong party on this round-trip voyage from New York to Havana obvious.

This ship is billed as a fantasy for those wealthy enough to afford it in these difficult times.

Before the repeal of Prohibition, the *Morro Castle*—named after the fortress guarding the Havana Harbor—offered an alcohol-filled cruise, where passengers could escape the dry streets and raging economic depression. Now that liquor is again legally available in the United States, the cruise's appeal hasn't lessened much. Thanks to the Labor Day holiday weekend, the pier is packed with guests in a celebratory mood.

There's a breeze in the air as Elena walks on deck, her dark brown hair whipping around her. Guests hang over the railing waving to friends and family on the dock below as though they will be separated for far longer than a week. But that's part of the adventure—the sensation that they are all embarking on uncharted territory, the voyage brimming with unlimited possibilities.

Elena leans over the railing herself, scanning the crowd. She's antsy for the ship to leave port, for the first part of her plan to tumble into motion. When they're at sea, far from land, they'll be in a cocoon that insulates them from real life and shrinks the world into a very small, manageable size.

It's the perfect hunting ground.

Elena abandons her perch at the rail and strolls around the deck, noting alcoves, spaces that are good for slipping away in case a hasty exit is needed. A few weeks ago, she went to the public library and found deck plans for the *Morro Castle*, poring over them as best she could. Still, there's nothing like walking the ship herself to get a feel for it and formulate these last, all-important parts of her plan.

Her prey is nowhere to be found, but no matter. On a ship this size, it will be impossible to escape.

Once she's examined the *Morro Castle*'s upper decks, Elena heads to her stateroom and closes the door behind her quickly.

The cabin is small and serviceable, the bed and mattress seemingly comfortable enough. It's not the nicest place she's ever slept, but it's also far from the worst. Her life has been a pendulum of comfort and insecurity, and for now she's just grateful to have a safe place to sleep.

She opens her suitcase, which one of the porters has already delivered to her room, and unpacks the worn clothes she brought for the cruise and the two dresses she bought for two very special occasions.

One is an emerald green color, elegant and fine. The other is a full-skirted blue number, daring and seductive, straps crisscrossed across the fitted bodice. It's a copy of a dress she once owned, each detail painstakingly re-created from memory.

She cannot wait to wear it.

Once Elena has finished unpacking, she exits her stateroom, locking the door behind her, and moves toward the belly of the ship, where the cargo is stored.

In her simple dress, her hair pulled back in a demure bun, no one looks twice at her. The clothes she wears have served her well as a disguise, each outfit presenting a different version of herself to the world, concealing her past and allowing her to navigate her present seamlessly.

The cargo hold is a cavernous space, filled with crates, trunks, and boxes, a faint smell of damp, metal, and sea life in the air. She moves through the room quickly, searching for one particular trunk, the hairpin she pulled to pick the lock resting in the pocket of her dress against her damp palm—

The sound of footsteps pierces the air.

She crouches behind a set of boxes piled as high as she is tall, peering around the corner.

A man strides toward the crates and trunks close to where Elena hides. He isn't dressed in the crew's distinctive uniforms, but rather clothes as nondescript and casual as hers. He's dark-haired and lean, young, too.

Elena pulls back. Better to return when the cargo hold is empty. Her foot catches on one of the boxes, and she lurches forward, crashing into the crate in front of her as she attempts to break her fall.

"Is someone there?" he calls out.

The entrance to the cargo hold is too far away for her to make it in time.

Heart pounding, Elena rises from her crouching position to her full height. "I'm sorry, I got lost. I didn't mean to interrupt your work—"

"—Just checking the cargo," he interjects easily. "Wanted to make sure everything that's supposed to be on the ship made it here safely. How did you get lost down here?"

He asks the question casually enough, but there's a hint there that suggests he's not as easygoing as he pretends to be. He speaks English with a familiar accent. He's Cuban, like her, and despite his claims that he was checking the cargo, the lack of official uniform and his intensity give the impression that he's as much a part of the crew as she is.

There are rumors of weapons being smuggled to Havana on the *Morro Castle*. Is he a smuggler?

"It's a big ship. I must have taken a wrong turn somewhere along the way," Elena answers.

"That's quite the wrong turn."

Her eyes widen with mock alarm, her heart pounding insistently in her breast. "You mean this isn't the ballroom?"

His lips curve slightly. "Perhaps I'm in the wrong place, then. Or at the very least, underdressed," he adds with a full smile.

She was told the hold would be unlocked at the beginning of the voyage, but whether it will remain that way once they leave port and the ship has set sail is another matter entirely. She could leave now and hope that when she returns later, he'll be gone and the trunk will still be here and accessible, or she can be honest—well, somewhat, at least. Years ago, the decision would have been simple, the urge to retreat practically second nature. But after everything she's been through, she's determined to be brave, and if now isn't the perfect opportunity to test out her newfound resolve, then when is?

"I need something from one of the trunks," she says, changing tack entirely.

"Do you now?"

"A friend sent me here," she adds, taking a chance. After all, Miguel is involved in various businesses in Cuba and the United States, the smuggling going on in this cargo hold likely bringing all manner of people together.

"A friend?" he counters.

"Yes." She hesitates. "Perhaps we have a mutual one."

His gaze turns speculative, and she can practically feel him mulling over the possibilities in his mind. "Perhaps we do. This friend of yours have a name?"

"Miguel." It's not much to go on, but if he knows Miguel

then he likely understands the importance of discretion—and loyalty.

He nods after a moment. "It seems we do have a friend in common. What do you need?"

"Something from that trunk," she replies, pointing to the container behind him.

"You're Cuban," he says.

"I am."

"And Miguel sent you to retrieve an item from that trunk?"

"No, I paid Miguel for an item in that trunk. He packed it for me."

"He mentioned that he was transporting something for a friend," the man answers. "I'll admit, I didn't anticipate someone like you being the 'friend' in question. I'll honor your deal with Miguel, but the rest of the contents in that trunk are mine."

"Of course. I have no interest in your business. This is a personal matter between me and Miguel."

He gestures at her with a sweep of his hand, indicating for her to walk ahead. "Be my guest. Any friend of Miguel's . . ."

His manner is friendly enough, but there's no question that he's in charge, and it feels as though he's luring her into a false sense of safety. After all, they're going to be trapped on this ship together for the next week, and were she foolish enough to expose the smuggling going on beneath the *Morro Castle*'s upper decks, then she'd have a target on her back for the remainder of the cruise.

He pulls a key out of his pants pocket and opens the trunk.

Elena takes a step forward, grateful she didn't have to try her hand with the hairpin.

A pistol rests on top of what looks to be an extensive cache of weapons inside the trunk. It's small enough to be easily concealed, but hopefully enough to satisfy her needs.

She grabs the gun, sliding it into the pocket of her skirt.

CHAPTER TWO

CATHERINE

When I was a little girl, my mother used to take me around New York City and show me the big, fancy buildings soaring high into the sky. We'd stand in front of them, and she'd arrange her fingers into the shape of a camera and pretend to take my picture. *Remember this moment, Katie!*

We called them our adventures, and on her rare days off when she wasn't cleaning up after the wealthy family she worked for, New York City was ours. We would roam the parts of the city we could, ogling the finery around us, staring into glass windows at beautiful gowns and out at sea, imagining all the places we could travel in a different life.

One day you'll go on a grand vacation. Just promise you'll take me with you, she would tease.

We couldn't afford the real thing, of course, but the pretense was nearly as good, and what I loved most about those memories was the way her lips would curve into a wide smile as though life was an adventure and one day our ship would come in and all our wildest dreams would come true.

In this moment in the New York Harbor, standing at Pier 13 on the gangway of the *Morro Castle*, the breeze blowing tendrils of hair from beneath my hat, it's as if she's standing before me, beaming down upon me, the ship grander than anything we could have ever imagined when I was a little girl.

Remember this moment, Katie!

Tears fill my eyes, and I bat them away, the enormous diamond ring on my left hand sparkling in the sunlight.

Overhead, towering above me like one of those great skyscrapers looming over the city skyline, the ship's horn blares, the sound echoing down the East River.

"Catherine, are you alright?" my fiancé Raymond asks beside me, his hand on my elbow holding me steady.

"Yes, I—" For a moment, my shoe slips, and I start once more, bumping into the gentleman in front of me.

"Pardon me—"

He turns swiftly, catching me off guard.

I'm used to the wealthy moving languidly, as though the world is to meet them on their timetable, but despite the fine cut of the man's coat, he's surprisingly quick, his dark eyes glancing from me to Raymond and back again before offering up a pretty apology, even though I'm the one who is responsible for our current contretemps.

My cheeks heat, the curse of my fair skin, and I take a deep breath, steadying myself until it all falls away—the luxurious black and white ocean liner, my handsome, elegant fiancé, the stranger I have jostled, the cheery crowds.

I am once again Catherine Dohan, a wealthy young heiress, unsettled by nothing, cowed by nothing, and I as much as the man in the fine suit in front of me belong here on the gangway of the *Morro Castle*, a lifetime of wedded happiness and comfort waiting for me.

It's a pretty lie, but a necessary one.

If my mother could only see me now.

Up ahead, a bellhop pushes the mountain of luggage for our little entourage—me, Raymond, Raymond's two-year-old daughter Ava, and her nanny—on the gangway leading to the ship.

I've never seen such a vessel in all my life. The rest of the first-class passengers appear nonplussed by the opulence, my fiancé included, so I adopt the bored expression so many of them favor, as though I was raised traveling all over the world, the *Morro Castle* just another ship in a long line of them.

It's a delicate balancing act to keep all the lies I've told straight, to keep everything from going up in flames.

Raymond escorts me to my cabin, leaving me to freshen up while he attends to some business on the ship. Ava's nanny has already taken her to the accommodations they'll share for the trip, the little girl fighting to keep her eyes open in the face of her regular nap time.

Once I feel refreshed, I meet Raymond for tea in the first-class lounge before we part ways and I find a comfortable spot on the sundeck to read. It's impossible to ignore the enthusiasm around me, to not feel a bit as though I am on the precipice of something new, to let some of that energy seep into my pores.

The child who dreamed of adventures would have given anything for a chance to sail on a ship such as this one, and the urge to commit every single detail to memory is overwhelming. The ship is spotless, and I can't help but wonder how difficult it must be to keep a vessel of this size clean and running smoothly. It certainly must be a gargantuan task.

It's a lively crowd on the *Morro Castle* today, particularly on A deck, everyone excited for our burgeoning adventure. I spy a few groups of women my age, laughing and talking together, and part of me yearns to go over and join them, to be myself rather than this fiction I have created.

I open my book instead.

I've learned that the best approach is to keep things simple, to stick to the truth—or a close approximation of it—as much as possible.

My official story is that I am an orphan now, as I am in real life, except that in the fiction, my deceased parents left me tremendous wealth rather than big dreams, memories of love, and nothing else.

Minutes pass by as I lie on deck, the afternoon sun strong.

I struggle to read; the sound of a nearby croquet game on deck pulls me out of my novel, the guests becoming uproariously loud as the play devolves into giggles and shouts.

"Nice ring."

I glance up as someone slides into the chair across from me.

It's the man from the gangway. The one with the quick reflexes that I bumped into.

It's forward of him to approach me without an introduction—even I know that—especially since I'm alone out here and he previously saw me in the company of my fiancé.

I don't bother responding, merely hold the book closer to my chest, peering over the top as I have seen so many society doyennes do, hoping I've successfully adopted their imposing stares with aplomb.

He lowers his smoke gray sunglasses to peer at me over the tops of his lenses.

His eyes, like his hair, are a dark brown.

"It's almost as beautiful as the woman wearing it," he adds, his lips curving into a flirtatious smile that lacks even a shred of genuineness.

What a truly atrocious line.

It isn't until his lips curve into real amusement, a startled laugh escaping his mouth, that I realize I've voiced the thought out loud.

"I'm reading," I add, too annoyed to be embarrassed by my directness, careful to keep my tone curt, hopeful he'll take the hint.

The last thing I need is for Raymond to see me in the company of another man, especially one as handsome as this one.

"*The Thin Man.*" He takes the book out of my hand and studies the cover. "Is it any good?" he asks, before returning it to me.

"I wouldn't know. I've barely had a chance to start it, considering all the interruptions."

His smile deepens. "I'm Harry."

"Hello, Harry. I am terribly sorry to be rude, but I really would like to get back to my novel. I'm sure it's quite fascinating."

I've always loved to read, probably for the same reasons I dreamed of adventure. There is freedom and excitement in slipping on other personas, in pretending to be someone you're not. When my mother taught me how to clean the immense mansion she cared for, I used to spend my days making up stories as I went about my chores, pretending I was the lady of the manor and envisioning the glamorous life I led.

In the evenings, I would read late into the night—books from the library that my employer's wife was kind enough to let me borrow—and those stories took me everywhere. I traveled back in time and to the future, across oceans and over mountains. I lived countless adventures in those books, and with each one I taught myself something about the world to be filed away for later use. Maybe I'd never been shopping in Paris, but I'd certainly read about characters who did so, making it easy enough when members of society questioned me, playing their little games to see if I really fit into their world.

Books made me who I am.

"What's the novel about?" Harry asks.

I know his type, could recognize it from across the cruise ship deck without batting an eye. He's a bounder, and an unapologetic one at that, and if I haven't judged him wrong—and I rarely do—he's on the make, his eyes a little too shrewd for the devil-may-care attitude he projects, his gaze more sharply attuned to the glint of my diamond ring than my feminine attributes. Perhaps he's hunting for a wealthy spouse as well, one of those unfortunate second sons left with little more than a good name, expensive tastes, and a need to make his way in the world. While I shouldn't fault him, given my own ambitions, I won't countenance anyone jeopardizing mine, and I doubt Raymond would take kindly to seeing me in the company of a young playboy.

"It's about a detective and his wife solving a mystery," I answer, my voice cold as ice.

"You like mysteries?"

"I like seeing people get what's coming to them."

His eyes widen slightly, and I instantly regret my words. There is a propensity among the wealthy to couch their feelings behind innuendo and a cutting sense of humor, and sometimes I forget my directness can get me in trouble. It's as much of a tell as using the wrong fork at dinner.

"I didn't know debutantes were so bloodthirsty." He looks like he's swallowing a laugh.

"Do you know many debutantes? Based on your behavior so far, I would have guessed married women were more your fare."

His eyes widen even more, and this time he doesn't even bother biting back a laugh that rolls over me, the rich sound making my toes curl, the invitation to arch my back and lean into the warm caress of that sound undeniable.

"I'm flattered you noticed," he teases.

"Don't be. I don't have the time or inclination for flirtations. Or the luxury."

For a moment I think he's going to offer another quip. He must see the sincerity in my words reflected in my expression, though, because he merely inclines his head to me before turning away, leaving me alone on my lounger on the deck, book in hand.

Each night, we are to dine formally, the *Morro Castle*'s chefs reputed to be extraordinary.

Now that the ship has made its way into the Atlantic Ocean, the rocking motions have grown more noticeable, and considering this is my first time at sea, my stomach roils and pitches as the evening progresses. And still, despite the threat of seasickness, there's something about the salt air, the hours spent on deck, that fills me with a tremendous hunger.

The *Morro Castle* in its stately grandeur is essentially an elegant hotel floating at sea. I lack the knowledge or interest to identify the style of decor other than to say it's vaguely European and reeking of wealth in an aspirational way I can't help but admire. As soon as you board the ship, you are treated as though you're royalty regardless of your station, even if there are subtle reminders—select social rooms reserved for first class and the like—that suggest otherwise. The *Morro Castle* isn't merely offering guests a vacation, it's creating an escape from the Depression, inviting passengers to leave the drudgeries of real life behind as they sail on this sumptuous voyage. Nowhere is that more personified than in the grand ballroom, where we are to dine this evening.

Raymond and I are led to our seats, wending our way through the ballroom. Raymond was delighted to be invited to the captain's table, the place of honor shared with several other guests for the evening. Unfortunately, the captain also chose to invite Harry, as well as a truly odious woman I saw berating her maid earlier in the hall. She's dressed in a garish green gown with ostrich plumes, an enormous emerald bracelet dangling from her right wrist.

The others at the table are already ensconced in conversation, Raymond and I the last to arrive. The volume drops slightly as we approach our dining companions and are introduced, as we are weighed and measured like pieces of meat.

I pass well enough under casual scrutiny, the engagement ring on my finger and Raymond on my arm doing the heavy lifting for me. The rest of it—the jewelry given to me by my fiancé, the dress borrowed from a stage production—good enough to satisfy most prying eyes.

I'm careful not to make eye contact with Harry as the waiter holds out my chair, Harry seated immediately to my left, the attention of our dinner companions fully shifting to us, the new arrivals.

Tonight, I opted for the emeralds Raymond bought me as an engagement gift, the ornate necklace the perfect accompaniment to the gown's low neckline.

This time when Harry's gaze drifts to me, I'm certain it isn't my jewelry he's ogling.

Despite his momentary shift in attention, he doesn't speak to me at all—perhaps he took my words to heart on the deck. His focus returns to the woman on his left—the one I saw lecturing her maid earlier.

Most of the dinner passes in silence for me as I listen to Raymond conversing with the other guests, his charm on full display. I realized a long time ago that in these situations, it's best to be circumspect, to let the others fill the table with their discussion, with their boasts and opinions. If I'm going to be found out, I imagine it will be in these moments when my guard is down, too busy focusing on proper dining etiquette, lulled into complacency by good food and wine.

In my silence, I learn Mrs. Gregory is eager to make a match for her daughter, and the possibility of a single gentleman like Harry seated so close by has inspired all her matchmaking fantasies. I can't help but chuckle at the fact that she seems more impressed by his outward appearance than she should be, and for someone who likely prides herself on being a reigning society queen, I'd expect her to have a better read on fortune hunters. Then again, it seems the male ones somehow always get a pass that isn't afforded to the rest of us similarly looking to improve our stations in life.

Her daughter sits to Mrs. Gregory's left, and already Mrs. Gregory has made several attempts to shift the seating arrangements to place Harry next to her daughter. I confess, the show going on before me is nearly as entertaining as any production the ship's social director could put on.

The food is as wonderful as promised, and by the time we've moved on to our entrées, Mrs. Gregory finally releases Harry from her clutches.

"That's a lovely necklace," Harry murmurs to me, Raymond's attention momentarily diverted by the captain, who has been regaling the other side of the table with stories of his adventures at sea.

I tilt my head, meeting Harry's gaze, the gleam in his eyes making it clear that he isn't talking about my necklace, but rather the décolletage it rests against.

"You're quite the jewelry aficionado," I drawl, unable to resist.

He grins. "Something like that. You need a matching bracelet. Emeralds."

"Perhaps *my fiancé* will give them to me as a wedding present."

"I imagine he will. Who wouldn't want to drape you in jewels?"

As far as lines go, it's hardly original and far too dramatic to be taken seriously.

"You flatter me," I murmur, spearing the peas on my plate with a fork.

Harry laughs, his voice low, his words for my ears alone. "No, I don't. That was another truly atrocious line." His tone is deadpan as he parrots my earlier words back to me.

I can't help but laugh. "True."

"Are you to be married on the ship?" Mrs. Gregory asks me, a touch too loudly to be polite, her voice making me jump, the pea skating across my plate.

"No, Raymond and I will be married when we return to New York City."

"And your family? Your parents? Surely, they accompanied you on this trip. Why, I can't imagine letting my daughter travel alone with her fiancé."

The aspersions she casts by suggesting there is something untoward with Raymond and me traveling together is quite neatly done, and I can't help but think it was her intention all along. We are hardly the only unmarried couple on the ship, and while none of it should be her concern, I've been around women like Mrs. Gregory my whole life and have seen the way they wield whatever they can to make others feel badly about themselves.

"My parents are deceased, sadly," I reply, staring down at

my plate to avoid letting the anger on my face show. "And we're hardly alone. Raymond's daughter Ava and her nanny are traveling with us. It's a family trip, you see."

"How terrible for you to lose your parents," Mrs. Gregory replies, ignoring my last words altogether. She's not concerned with where my life is headed—she wants to know where I've been, who I am, where I come from. "Were you quite young when it happened?"

There's nothing outwardly rude about her questions, but there's something in her manner that pins me to my chair like an insect trapped beneath a magnifying glass. This woman will have my secrets by the dessert course if she has her way.

"Young enough. Is there ever an age where the loss of a parent is easy? I am sure your own dear daughter would be devastated to lose you."

I say it with a pleasant enough smile, no hint of a threat in my voice, but there's enough of an edge there, I hope, to send a message—

I am not to be trifled with.

Beside me, Harry coughs into his napkin and I get the sensation that he's trying not to laugh again.

"Perhaps we should change the conversation to more agreeable things," Raymond suggests, his attention finally diverted from the captain's nautical tales. "I have no wish to upset my young bride on what is to be a relaxing voyage."

"Of course," Mrs. Gregory replies smoothly, even though

she's likely already formulating the next set of questions in her mind. She seems like the sort of woman who spends her time occupied with everyone else.

She raises her hand, her fork filled with fish.

I blink.

The emerald bracelet she was wearing earlier is now gone.

I open my mouth to say something, but Raymond chooses that moment to ask me a question, and I turn my attention toward him and the captain, the bracelet drifting from my mind.

When we're finished dining, Raymond and I excuse ourselves from the table.

"Do you want to check on Ava?" I ask him.

"No. I'm sure she's fine with Emily."

It's taken a bit to get used to the way the wealthy parent their children; Ava's nanny Emily is with her far more than Raymond ever is, and even though I am engaged to her father, the two-year-old and I have spent little time together despite my attempts to include her in our burgeoning life together. My childhood was so defined by my mother's love and influence despite the long hours she worked that it is unfathomable to me that a parent could be so distant from their own child, especially one as young as Ava.

"Are you sure? She must miss you."

"Don't be silly. She's probably already sleeping," he replies, his tone as dismissive as it always is when I broach the topic of

Ava. She's not my child, but I can't help but worry about her well-being.

There's a chill in the air from the ocean breeze when we reach the open deck, and I wrap my shawl more tightly around my shoulders, grateful for the comfort it provides.

Raymond pats his dinner jacket and frowns. "I think my cigarette case is back in my stateroom. I'll be right back."

He leaves me standing alone on the deck, the moon shining over the midnight water, the faint sound of the band's music escaping from the ballroom. I walk toward the railing, staring out at the ocean. I lean forward and take another deep breath, and then another. The voice I've mostly silenced creeps back in my head, the worry and fear that I will slip up, that this is too big of a reach. Then I remember why I am doing this, how much is at stake if I succeed, and, well, how can I not try with everything I have? In for a penny, in for a pound, as they say.

Footsteps on the deck behind me have me turning around swiftly, but where I expected to see Raymond returning with his elegant gold cigarette case in hand, I am greeted instead by a couple enjoying a romantic midnight stroll. They incline their heads to me before passing by, their laughter trailing behind them.

I glance back at the ocean, the sea forming white, foamy caps as the large vessel charges through the water. The size of the ship is even more noticeable considering the presence it has in the sea, even if the vastness surrounding us provides the illusion that we are all alone on this floating paradise. Out here, away from the glittering chandeliers and dazzling jewels, it's easy to feel as though I have escaped to another world, as though there is solace in the roar of the ocean, the endless sky of stars. I close my eyes, and for a moment, it all slips away, the layers I have heaped on top of myself to carve a space in this cutthroat society, and in this instant I am free.

I don't think I've been anywhere this beautiful in all my life.

The sound of footsteps once again breaks into my reverie, a faint whiff of cigarette smoke behind me, and I stifle the sigh that rises inside of me, that little huff of annoyance at Raymond interrupting the solitude of this moment. Like a coat I slip on over my fine gown, I affix a smile on my face as I turn away from the stunning view before me.

It isn't Raymond standing in front of me.

The man moves so swiftly he's little more than a blur, and then his hands are at my neck, his fingers pressing into my skin, squeezing, pushing me back against the ship's railing, the cold metal digging into my spine through the layers of my evening gown. I open my mouth to scream, but the man's hands at my throat cut off all sound. I gasp for air, clawing at his fingers, gripping his hairy wrists to no avail. A wave of dizziness overcomes me, the edges of my vision darkening, and instinctively, I do as my mother taught me when I was a young girl—

There will be men who try to take advantage of you, Katie, and when they do, you go for where you can hurt them the most.

I pull my knee up hard, connecting with the man's groin.

He doubles over, a curse falling from his lips, and it's enough to get his hands off my neck, for him to take a step back, and another. There's only a moment of respite, for the fresh air to seep into my lungs, and then he reaches into his trench coat—

I move instinctively now, lunging toward him, my hand closing over his, resting on the hilt of a gun. It happens so quickly that I barely register what direction the gun is pointing or whose finger is mashed against the trigger. It must be mine, though, because there's a shot and the man falls to the deck floor, a red stain blooming on his white shirt.

CHAPTER THREE

The man lies on the ship's deck before me. He hasn't moved since the gun went off—

I raise my hands to my throat, gingerly touching the spot where he grabbed me, the skin already sore. Did he mean to take my necklace? The emeralds are certainly attention-grabbing, but his grip was higher than where the stones rest on my chest, the necklace still intact.

He was going for my throat.

My knees shake and I grip the railing, trying to steady myself.

I scan the deck quickly. There's no one around, the sound of the band playing music so loud that it spills out onto the deck.

Think.

Raymond will be back soon.

He can't find me like this.

I lean forward and place my fingers on the side of the man's neck, searching for a pulse there.

My fingers tremble as they brush against his bare skin.

Nothing.

He's dead.

Damn it.

What do I do now?

The gun rests next to him on the ground, and I pick it up, my hands acting so quickly my mind barely has time to keep up as I toss the gun over the side of the ship, watching as it makes a small splash in the vast ocean below. If only the body was so easily disposed of—

"Am I interrupting something?"

I turn slowly, my mind racing as I attempt to conjure a plausible explanation for the dead body beside me.

Harry's eyes widen as he stares down at the man on the ground, all traces of humor momentarily wiped from his expression.

A low whistle escapes his lips. "Well, you're certainly in trouble now."

"It's not what it looks like."

I can barely recognize the sound of my own voice, the sharp pitch of panic as unfamiliar to me as the situation that I find myself in.

"It looks like you shot a man." He says the words surprisingly calmly given the circumstances. A more nervous—or prudent—man might take a step back or two, but Harry remains where he is, his feet firmly planted on the deck.

"He attacked me."

Harry's eyes narrow slightly. "What do you mean 'attacked you'?"

I take a deep breath, panic building as I remember the feel of the man's hands on my body. "He tried to rob me, I think. He had a gun."

"Where is the gun now?"

I hesitate. "I threw it overboard."

"Quick thinking."

"It's not—it's not like that. I didn't know what to do. I panicked."

"How do you mean to get rid of the body?"

Raymond will return any moment. It doesn't take that long to walk back from his cabin. There's only one place I can think of to make the man disappear for good.

"If he went overboard—It's so loud tonight, what with everyone partying and the band playing. I don't think anyone would notice the splash. It's not like anyone has run out here because of the gunshot," I reply.

"There's no chance of you getting that body over the rails."

"I know that. Help me. Please."

My fake identity might fool a few guests at dinner, but there's no way it will hold up under law enforcement's scrutiny, and I'm not the sort of person who fares well when the police start sniffing around. I've seen enough to know how the poor are treated.

"'Please'? We've certainly gotten off to a new start. Why, earlier today, you would barely acknowledge me, and now you're asking me to hide a dead body for you."

"Not 'hide'—throw overboard," I remind him. "Which is why I require your assistance."

"See, that's where I start wondering 'why me?' Don't you have a fiancé who is ready and willing to ride in and rescue a damsel in distress?" He shoots me a frank look. "Although not quite a damsel and not-so-in-distress."

"He was trying to kill me."

"So you say, but right now all I have to go on is a dead body with a hole in his chest and a beautiful woman who, if you don't mind me saying, seems a little secretive. Who was he to you? Scorned lover? Bill collector? Jealous husband?"

"Don't be ridiculous. I have absolutely no idea who he was. I came out here to get some air, and he tried to rob me. He put his hands around my neck."

Harry's gaze drifts to my skin.

"It's red." His voice tightens. "You'll probably have a bruise tomorrow."

I'll have to use makeup to cover it up. Another benefit of my short-lived acting career—I never worked on productions that had large enough budgets to hire a full staff, so I learned how to do my own makeup, adapting my needs to the role I was playing.

"I told you. We struggled over the gun, and I, well—"

I can't say the words *I shot him* aloud, for if I do, it will make all of this real, and I fear the tenuous grasp I have on my emotions will simply crash down around me.

My teeth chatter, shock settling in.

"—You shot him," Harry finishes.

"Please just help me. Before anyone else comes out here and sees us."

"Dispose of a dead body? You have a lot of nerve. Why would I make myself an accessory to murder for a stranger? Maybe you're used to men doing your bidding, and I'm not saying you're not gorgeous, but I'm not stupid. I have no desire to spend the rest of my days in a jail cell. Especially risking my neck for someone else."

"It wasn't murder," I snap. "It was self-defense. And some men help a lady because they're gentlemen."

"Well, you're out of luck, here, I am not a gentleman, evening clothes be damned, and there's no chance I'm going to haul this poor sod over the railing for you."

"Fine, just leave me alone, then."

"Well, now my curiosity is piqued, how do you propose to get him over the railing on your own?"

I take a step toward the body, and then another, trying to avert my gaze from the bloody hole in his chest, my heart pounding. This part of the ship seems more remote at this hour, but how long do we have before a crew member comes over here, or one of the other guests, perhaps on an assignation of their own? Or what if Raymond returns? How can I explain this scene to him?

I grab one of the dead man's legs, wincing at the heft. Do dead bodies weigh more than live ones? It surely feels as though they do.

Harry pushes off from the railing. "I think this is my cue to leave. At this rate, you'll be caught in five minutes."

I stare at his retreating back, fury filling me.

"I saw you take that bracelet at dinner," I call after him, bluffing out of desperation.

He stops walking.

"I wonder what the ship's officials would think if I told them," I add. "I'm sure Mrs. Gregory is very upset about her missing jewels."

He pivots around slowly. "I don't know what you're talking about."

"Please. It was blatantly obvious."

He looks vaguely affronted.

"The only reason *she* didn't notice was that ridiculous drivel you were spouting."

"Her eyes really do resemble emeralds," he retorts.

"Yes, that must have been why she chose that bracelet you stole. You can help me right now. Get rid of this fellow in exchange for my silence. Otherwise, I'll go straight to the authorities."

It's a gamble but faced with the alternative, it's all I have.

Harry closes the distance between us so quickly that if I'd blinked, I would have missed it. He moves gracefully for such a big man—light on his feet with a sort of panther-like agility.

Are his escapades limited to broad daylight or does he use these skills climbing into windows and the like?

"You're a thief," I challenge, taking a wild guess that suddenly fits with all my observations about him.

"So, what if I am?" He shrugs. "You're running a scam of your own. I pegged it as soon as I saw you on that gangway. Your eyes were as wide as saucers looking up at that ship. Have you ever even been on a boat before?"

My cheeks heat. If he noticed, who else did?

"Have you?" I counter.

"It's where I do my best work. Now, though, only one of us is responsible for a dead body, so I'll take my chances. Go ahead and say something; Mrs. Gregory hasn't even noticed. They would have sounded the alarm if she had, and who's to say it won't be right back on her wrist before they get a chance to investigate?"

"You couldn't pull that off without her noticing."

He grins. "You have no idea."

"This isn't a game," I hiss.

"Life is a game. Business is a game. Love is a game. It all is. Maybe you're losing because you take things too seriously. Or you just haven't found the right person to play with."

"Who says I'm losing? I'm the one with a diamond ring on my finger."

"And a dead man at your feet."

"He wouldn't be dead if he hadn't attacked me."

His gaze narrows speculatively. "Strange, isn't it, that he would attack you?"

"What's that supposed to mean?"

"Just that I can think of smarter places to commit a crime than a cruise ship, where there's little hope of escape and few opportunities to hide."

"And yet, you're here."

"Touché. And still, it seems like a brazen crime given our present circumstances."

"Or you could argue that a cruise ship is the perfect place to commit a crime. After all, it's a controlled hunting ground with limited opportunities for your prey to escape and an endless ocean at the ready to dispose of any evidence. Perhaps he was planning on disembarking in Havana."

"Perhaps."

"Besides, one can hardly account for the rash decisions men make. Maybe he was a stupid thief and didn't think his plan through all that well."

"Maybe he wasn't a thief at all. Maybe you were lucky you shot him."

"What's that supposed to mean?"

He shrugs. "Just saying, speaking from professional experience, it doesn't make a lot of sense. Look at his clothes for one—he's well dressed. Not the look of a man who is desperate enough to attack a woman and rob her in a confined space such as this one."

"He could have stolen the clothes."

"If he did, then he just happened to find a man who had exactly his measurements. That's some remarkable luck right there. I know tailors, and his suit looks tailored."

"I'd prefer if we focused on getting his suit overboard rather than critiquing his sartorial style."

"Then you'd better help me lift him, because I'm not wrenching my back over this mess."

I lean down, taking the man's feet while Harry walks over and grabs under the man's armpits.

"His shoes are nice, too," I murmur to myself.

You learn a lot about shoes when you're forced to wear the same pair several sizes past their prime. These are not the cheap, worn material of my childhood, but a fancy black leather pair barely broken in.

Could Harry be right? Could the robbery have been less random than it seemed?

"On three," Harry says through gritted teeth. "We'll lift him and haul him over."

"Wait—what if I can't lift him?"

"Then you're going to have a hell of a time explaining this."

An oath slips past my lips.

It takes a few tries, but eventually we both hoist him up, and I'm grateful for whatever stroke of luck had the man attack me so close to the rail. There's no way we'd be able to drag him much farther.

"You sure you want to do this?" Harry asks me, grunting at the weight of the body between us.

Maybe law enforcement would be assuaged by the fact that I am a "lady" and do little more than a cursory investigation, but what if they aren't? What if they dig into my background? What if Raymond finds out about my past?

"I'm sure."

We lift the man up until his body is braced across the top of the deck rail, and then with one clumsy shove, and another, he's tipped over into the sea, lost to the dark night.

For a moment, neither one of us speaks, our gazes trained to the water below. I've gotten my hands dirty a time or two in life, but this is a new experience for me, and I've no doubt that when I return to my cabin this evening, a stiff drink will be in order. For his part, Harry doesn't look much better.

I glance down. There's a red spot on the deck. And on the railing.

"He bled," I hiss. "What are we going to do now?"

"There's not much we can do. The crew is meticulous about keeping the ship immaculate. Haven't you noticed how they're constantly painting over scuff marks on the deck? Someone will come and think a guest had a minor accident, and they'll clean it up. It's the best we can hope for."

"And if they don't? If they decide it looks suspicious and investigate?"

"Did anyone see you out here?"

"Raymond was with me earlier. He went back to the cabin to get his cigarette case. There was a couple that walked by a little after that as well."

"If it were me, I'd head Raymond off before he makes his

way back here. Everyone's been drinking; he probably won't remember the exact place that he left you. And if the couple saw you from a distance—well, they might not remember, either."

"That's a lot of luck to hope for."

"What else are you going to do?"

He has a point there.

Harry holds out a small, dark object to me.

"What's that?" I ask.

"His wallet. I took it from him before we hoisted him up. If it were me, I'd want to know a little more about a man who tried to attack me."

"I think I'd prefer not to know anything about him."

Harry lifts the wallet over his head—

"—Wait. What was his name? Just tell me that."

"Mark Reynolds," Harry replies after he opens the wallet, flicking through the information there.

"I don't know any Mark Reynolds. Maybe it was just a random attack."

"Maybe." Harry's silent for a moment. "For him to attack you on the ship like this—" He hesitates. "Just be careful."

He tosses the wallet overboard.

Harry gives me a little nod and then he turns away from me, leaving me standing alone on the deck, staring after his retreating back.

I glance down.

Mrs. Gregory's missing emerald bracelet is draped on my wrist.

ELENA

The moonlight shines down on the deck of the *Morro Castle*, and Elena waits, watches, the lone bystander to the death that just occurred, the sound of her breaths swallowed by the roar of the wind and the waves.

She came out just as they began struggling for the gun, her heart pounding.

She almost emerged from the shadows after the gunshot, but then the man arrived and the pair began arguing over what to do about the body.

Long after they are gone, traces of blood on the deck, she remains hidden in the dark, her gaze cast to the ocean as though she could somehow make out the features of the man they dumped overboard in the inky night and crashing seas, as though she could somehow untangle all that has happened and make sense of it, altering the situation as needed.

His body has been swept away, but what has just happened changes everything, of course—

A sleek dart of fear fills her, a tremor sliding down her body, and in its wake, fury settles in.

CHAPTER FOUR

CATHERINE

The purloined bracelet burns a hole in my evening bag.

I did as Harry suggested and headed for Raymond's state-room, running into him in the hallway. I told him I wasn't feeling well, that I had decided to retire for the evening, wrapping my shawl tightly around my shoulders and chest, hoping it covered the redness on my neck and would stave off any questions my fiancé might have.

I then went to a member of the crew and passed them a tip, asking for Harry's cabin number.

Who knows what he intended when he put the bracelet on my wrist, but if Mrs. Gregory has reported it missing and I'm caught with it—

I stop in front of Harry's cabin, my heart pounding as I do a quick sweep of the hallway. I've noticed the staff likes to make several passes by the staterooms in case they should need to come to a guest's assistance, and as much as I've attempted to find a rhythm to their movements, they don't seem to follow a set schedule or pattern.

For now, though, the hallway is clear, the other guests hopefully otherwise entertained with the various revels offered on the ship. I'd prefer to get this business over as quickly and painlessly as possible.

I knock on Harry's stateroom door, praying it's too early in the evening for him to have returned to his cabin. He's likely enjoying the multitude of entertainments the cruise has to offer.

The evening's events have left me more unsettled than I'd like to admit, the memory of that man's hands around my neck firmly imprinted on my mind. Hours ago, I looked out at the vast ocean and saw freedom. Now, I see potential threats around each corridor, the fear that it will be my body heading over that railing next.

When Harry doesn't answer, I pull a hairpin out of my coiffure and place it in front of the cabin's keyhole, using it like the boys in our apartment building taught me so many years ago.

It takes longer than I remember, but eventually it comes back to me—like riding a bicycle, they say—and the lock tumbles open.

I glance down the corridor in each direction before turning the knob and entering Harry's room, shutting the door behind me quickly.

He's left a light on in his cabin, hopefully not because he's planning on returning soon. The bed is unmade, a dinner jacket discarded on the sofa, a pair of gleaming black loafers kicked underneath the desk, a silk dressing gown draped over the edge of the bed.

His room couldn't be more different than mine. I've left my stateroom neat as a pin, a lifetime of living in cramped quarters impressing upon me the importance of keeping an orderly living space. Harry's stateroom looks like he's left his mark on every square inch that he could find.

I freeze at the sound of a key in a lock.

My gaze darts around the room, struggling to think of a place I can hide, how I can avoid the awkwardness of having to admit that I snuck into his cabin. I'm halfway to the bathroom when the door to the stateroom swings open.

Damn.

Harry stops in his tracks.

In the natural space where I would fill the silence with some explanation as to *why* I am in his cabin, I opt to instead meet his gaze, holding it defiantly.

After all, we would never be in this position if he hadn't stolen the blasted bracelet in the first place.

He closes the door behind him, and leans against it, effectively blocking my exit, a grin on his face.

He looks a little rough around the edges—as though he's been out and up to some form of debauchery or another in the time since we last saw each other. The faint whiff of cigar smoke and whiskey catches my nose.

"Back so soon? Is there another dead body you need help with? Or dare I hope you're here for a late-night rendezvous?"

"Hardly."

"Hey, don't knock it until you've tried it. I've been told I have a knack with my hands."

"Oh, I believe it," I reply, holding the bracelet out to him. "I'm just not interested. In *that* or Mrs. Gregory's bracelet."

"That's a shame." He steps closer, taking the bracelet from me. "It looked good on your wrist."

"It did; jewels tend to have that effect. But it was hardly good enough considering the risk."

"Is that what you do—weigh risk and reward when you make your decisions?"

"Isn't that what everyone does?"

"Surely emotion factors into your decisions somewhat," he replies, ignoring my question.

"Some emotions. Loyalty, friendship."

"Very noble emotions."

"You're mocking me."

"I'm not. Merely curious to understand you better. I confess, I had sort of written you off as being largely uninteresting when I saw you boarding the ship with your fiancé and later on the deck. Fascinating jewelry collection, of course, but not much beyond the surface."

"Do you usually have much success with women?" I ask, more than a little affronted by being described as "largely uninteresting."

"I always have success with women." He shrugs. "It's clear you know the effect you have on others. I'm not going to waste my time padding your vanity with useless, pretty words. You and I have seen the truth of each other, now haven't we, after that little business on the deck? Hardly seems necessary to pretend we're something we're not."

"But that's what you're doing on this ship, isn't it—pretending? Don't you think it's a bit rash to steal from a woman you just ate dinner with? When did you take it, after all?"

"So, you didn't see me do it, and you just noticed it missing at one point. I wondered if you were bluffing when you tried to blackmail me on the deck or if I was losing my touch." He chuckles. "Upset you missed it? Worried you're losing your edge considering all the little things happening on this ship right underneath your nose?"

"What's that supposed to mean?"

"You're not just beautiful. You're smart. You spoke little at dinner this evening, and maybe you can convince some people that you're shy or demure, but it's not that at all. You watch everyone at the table like you're playing poker. You watch your fiancé like that, too."

"Every woman should watch her fiancé like that," I mutter under my breath.

He chuckles again. "I bet you're hell at a poker table."

"I wouldn't know. I've never played. My mother didn't approve of gambling. She didn't approve of stealing, either."

No doubt she looked the other way in our leaner years when she was unemployed, when I would do what I could on the streets to survive. That—I understand. The kind of need to survive that pushes you to do whatever it takes. But Harry is too finely dressed for all that, too comfortable for me to believe that he's on the precipice of ruin. So, what is it that pushes him to steal and enables him to still be able to meet his own gaze in the mirror? I find that the tenets my mother tried so hard to instill in me stick, whether I want them to or not, and it's difficult to not feel weighed down by the knowledge that she would likely be disappointed by the crooked path my life has taken— even if I pray she would understand the reasons for it.

"Is that a faint note of disapproval I hear in your voice?" Harry asks.

I shrug. "Take it however you like. It just seems like you're asking for trouble by so blatantly stealing from another dinner guest, even one as odious as Mrs. Gregory."

"Would it make you feel better if I gave the bracelet to the waiter she was so unconscionably rude to? Lord knows the man deserves it and more for having to put up with that woman. And I'll have you know I took it off her right before dessert was served. When she nearly made you cry."

"She did not make me cry. She made me angry."

"It was more than that; I saw it on your face. She made you sad and I didn't like that."

"So, because someone made me sad, you're willing to risk your freedom? I find that very hard to believe, and if that is the sort of risk and reward calculation that you do, then I greatly fear for your ability to survive in this world."

"Do you?"

"I do."

"Then let me assuage you with this. She'll never know I took the bracelet. I've been doing this long enough to promise you that. And I took it because it kept an interminable dinner filled with smug people from being a complete and total loss."

"I assure you, a woman knows if she loses a bracelet like this."

"Maybe you would because you seem as though you count everything you have at least twice, but Mrs. Gregory will be convinced it fell off on the ship somewhere—after all, she complained that the clasp kept catching on her gown—and be too embarrassed to tell her husband she lost the jewelry. He probably wouldn't care anyway because he likely bought his mistress a similar piece, which adorns her wrist in the villa in Nice where they're currently vacationing while his daughter and wife enjoy this little diversion."

"That's quite the vivid description you've conjured up. What if you're wrong about all of it? What if she will miss the bracelet? What if she remembers that handsome young man paying a great deal of attention to it? Or if she blames someone else for the theft?"

"Then the bracelet will miraculously appear in her cabin, and she will certainly be embarrassed—not for the fuss she caused and the pain she inflicted on an innocent person, but because then she would be wrong, and women like Mrs. Gregory above all else do not like to be wrong. And I wasn't paying a great deal of attention to it; I was paying a great deal of attention to *you*. Perhaps there was only one thing at that table I truly wanted to steal, and it wasn't the bracelet."

"Now I know you're speaking absolute nonsense. I cannot be stolen. Nor do I wish to be. And you shouldn't say such things anyway. I am an engaged woman."

"So, you say."

"What is that supposed to mean?"

"Just that I know a thing or two about pretending to be something you're not. From one pretender to another, you're not as good as you think you are. I'd bet a great deal that you aren't really an heiress and that your engagement is more of a pecuniary matter than an emotional one."

"And you're not as invincible as you think you are, so you should be more discreet with your activities," I snap, more than a little incensed by the notion that he has so swiftly gotten to the heart of things and seen me for who I am rather than who I wish the world believes me to be. A man who knows my secrets is a truly dangerous obstacle now, and in that little reveal, Harry just elevated himself from nuisance to adversary.

"There must be something truly perverse in me that I feel

a little tingle at the base of my spine when you scold me. It's a beautiful thing," he teases. "I think I like it even more than you referring to me as a 'handsome young man.'"

I roll my eyes. "Are you ever serious? Is everything just a game to you? A constant flirtation? It must be nice to be so carefree with your life while others foot the bill."

"Life is too serious to be taken seriously. I learned that lesson a long time ago. And do you think Mrs. Gregory earned this emerald bracelet through hard work—hers or her husband's—or is it far more likely that they just happened to be born into the right house, to the right families, and coast on that for the rest of their lives? There's an economic depression going on, not that they'd know it."

"You could say that about many on this ship, yourself included. I wouldn't know, nor would I particularly pretend to care about the Gregory family. They're of no use to me. I learned to look out for myself and not to let anything or anyone get in the way of that."

"Is that a threat?" he asks, a note of amusement in his voice.

Fine, let him underestimate me. It's not the first time and I doubt it will be the last.

"No, it's a promise. Don't go repeating what you just said about me again."

"The part about you not being an heiress? I wouldn't dream of it. I don't know what your grift is exactly, but from one scoundrel to another, I'm just here to enjoy the show. Besides, the more trouble you cause, the more distracted the guests will be from *my* activities." He grins. "Have I ever told you how much I like a challenge? There's nothing like the rush I get when I lift a piece of jewelry off someone. I have a feeling I'm going to like the challenge of getting under your skin."

"You're welcome to try, but I assure you—you won't be successful. You aren't the first scoundrel to show an interest in me and I'm sure you won't be the last, so pardon me if I'm not on tenterhooks waiting to see what you do next. Just keep your jewelry to yourself, because next time I find a bracelet belonging to another guest on my wrist, I just might turn you in to the ship's staff."

"You wouldn't. We're partners in crime now, remember? Our fates were bound together when we chucked that man's body overboard."

"He deserved it."

"He likely did. In my experience, people don't get what they deserve often enough."

"I have to agree with you there," I mutter.

"See, we have more in common than you think. You don't suffer fools. One of the regrettable downsides of my line of work is how solitary it is. I can't tell you how intriguing it is to have finally found an interesting match."

"Your entertainment is hardly my concern."

"Your loss, then."

I leave his stateroom without another word, the emerald bracelet in his hands once more.

CHAPTER FIVE

ELENA

She sleeps on a soft mattress, the silk sheets smooth against her skin. It's warm tonight, and somewhere in the recesses of her mind it occurs to her that she should ask one of the staff to open a window, let some breeze into her bedroom. It's too stifling in this house, too oppressive. For all the finery that surrounds her, sometimes it feels as if she's trapped in a mausoleum. It's a far cry from the fantasies she had when she first saw the mansion in the city, when she imagined the home it would become, the laughter that would fill its drafty rooms. She envisioned babies born, children running down the halls, a lifetime lived.

She thought she'd finally have the family she desperately craved.

There's no laughter now, only a whiff of fear that lies around each corner.

If she were more fanciful, less practical, she would swear that the house was trying to kill her—the raised nail on the staircase that she tripped on nearly falling to her death, the loose chandelier, the tipped-over candlestick that started a fire a few weeks ago, the list of the mansion's perfidies grows. And still, the accidents continue.

She coughs, turning to her side, flinging off the covers, the heat becoming unbearable now. Is she ill? She was weeks ago, something from the house's kitchen not sitting well with her, leaving her feverish, her stomach cramping painfully. She was sick for days.

Hands shake her.

She moans.

"Wake up. The house is on fire."

Elena jolts out of bed, staring up at the ceiling, a thin sheen of sweat covering her body.

It's been a year, and the sight of fire, the smell of smoke, still sends a tremor down her spine, filling her with terror.

She casts the sheets off, rising from the bed, anger filling her at the dampness in the linens from the sweat that has come off her body. It's the weakness that bothers her most, the way in which her ghosts still haunt her no matter how hard she tries to overcome the past. It's a weakness she can't afford, especially now, with all her plans so close to fruition.

She dresses quickly, desperate for fresh air and freedom from the stifling cabin.

Her heart rate doesn't slow until she's on the deck, a light breeze in the air, the sound of the music from the party going on indoors drifting out into the moonlight. It's late or early, depending on your perspective, but time shifts on a ship like this, the guests enjoying the festivities all day and all night long.

It's dangerous being out here, risking being recognized, but after the nightmare, she can't imagine going back to the cabin and sitting alone while her fears get the best of her. Sometimes it takes hours after one of her dreams for her to settle down to a place where she can fall asleep again.

Elena walks over to the railing, her back to the guests partying inside, the familiar strands of a song she once danced to years ago nearly making her weep, the memories it conjures up transporting her to a simpler time, a happier one, when she was loved and safe.

And then she can't resist the urge, abandoning her place at the railing and turning toward the dancing, peering inside the open window to watch the guests whirling around and around, their laughter filling the ballroom.

The sound of footsteps echo behind her.

She turns, her heart pounding.

The man from the cargo hold walks toward her.

"Mind if I join you?" he asks.

The instinct to tell him she does mind is on the tip of her tongue, but then again, the dream is still fresh and it's dangerous being out here alone like this. Better to have a witness if there is trouble, even if she isn't entirely sure he doesn't bring his own set of entanglements.

"Sure."

"I'm Julio," he says, introducing himself. "You know, you never told me your name back there—in the cargo hold."

She hesitates for a moment, torn between the desire to lie and the simplicity of honesty. She kept her first name unchanged in her identification documents because it seemed easier that way—less confusion with all the stories she was meant to keep straight in her head. It's a common enough name, hardly sufficient to raise suspicion, yet the desire to be wary is there regardless.

Once upon a time, she trusted the wrong person, and look how that turned out.

"Elena."

"It's nice to properly meet you, Elena."

He jerks his head back toward the direction of the music that has grown even louder in the last few minutes. "You aren't joining the party?" he asks, even though he's dressed as casually as she is. "I see you finally found your way to the ballroom," he adds, referring to her earlier quip in the cargo hold.

She can't help but smile. "No—I'm not much for formal occasions."

That's not entirely true, of course. Once she would have been at home in the ballroom, draped in the same gowns that now pass by her as she stands in the shadows peering in. In a past life, she would have been thrilled for an event such as this.

"You were sure watching intently for someone who isn't interested."

"What about you? Were you planning on joining the festivities?"

He shrugs. "I just came out for a smoke. I'm not one for parties and I left my tuxedo back in Havana."

"Do you spend much time in New York?"

"Occasionally. I have some family there and I visit them when I can, when I'm traveling for business. Where is home for you?"

"I don't really have one now. You could say I travel a lot, too."

"But you're Cuban?"

"I was born in Havana, yes. I haven't lived there for a long time, though."

Suddenly, the guests in the ballroom break out into raucous laughter, and she turns her attention away from Julio, looking through the glass once more.

"They'll only be able to hold this facade together for so long," he muses.

"What do you mean?"

"There's trouble in paradise. With the crew."

"What sort of trouble?"

"They're unhappy with how they're treated on the ship. Some say the captain is afraid of a mutiny. It's hard finding a good crew. The wages aren't great, the hours long, the turnover high. They're perpetually short on the number of bodies it takes to run the *Morro Castle*. That's why it's easy to get someone to look the other way if you know the right incentive."

"And what is the right incentive?" she asks.

"Money. Always money. No one ever has enough of that these days."

The effects of the economic depression are being felt all over the world, influencing things in Havana, too.

"That's how you get the weapons to Cuba. You bribe someone to let you bring them aboard the ship."

"You'd be surprised. There are many factors at play when it comes to Cuba. Those weapons come down from more official channels than you'd think. How do you know Miguel?" he asks her, changing the subject.

"From Havana. We grew up together. We reconnected in New York."

"He's a good man."

"He is. How long have you been doing this?" she asks, more out of curiosity than anything else.

"Long time. Since the *Morro Castle* started its runs from New York to Havana. It's not too bad, although some of the officers and crew don't take as kindly to it as others. There's only so much money for bribes. You must be careful about who you offer them to."

"It sounds like a dangerous line of work."

"What isn't dangerous these days? At least, it's being done for a good cause."

She remembers enough of the violence in Havana when she was a little girl, despite her parents' best efforts to shield her from it, to know that it feels as though there has always been fighting in Cuba, will always be a battle for freedom.

"What do you want more than anything?" he asks her.

She doesn't even think about her response, the dream so fresh in her mind that the word slips out as if of its own volition.

"Revenge."

If he's surprised by her answer, he doesn't give any indication, but then again, the gun probably tipped him off.

"And what happens if you get your revenge? What comes after that? It seems to me that if you dedicate your life to hating someone or something, then they've already won."

"That's funny advice coming from a man who is shipping weapons and trying to support a revolution."

"My revolution isn't for revenge. It's because I believe in a better future for my country."

"And maybe I believe the world will be a better place when I have my revenge. Safer, at least, for sure."

"Then you must have a dangerous adversary."

"I do. A powerful one, which is the most dangerous kind."

"I'm glad Miguel is helping you. He's good at that—at evening the odds. It's difficult when the threat you face seems insurmountable."

"I'm a woman. I've spent most of my life feeling that way. I assure you, at some point that sensation becomes such a part of you that you hardly think of it as a barrier at all. In fact, it can be your greatest advantage because if they underestimate you—"

"—They don't see you coming," Julio finishes for her.

She smiles. "Exactly."

"Will you have your revenge on this ship?"

"Hopefully. Or I'll die trying."

"Then I wish you well. I know a thing or two about lost causes and it's hard to not cheer for David when they go up against Goliath."

"That is a remarkably apt description."

For so long, she has gone about the world feeling as though she cannot trust others, looking over her shoulder, wary of strangers. But there's something nice about being in the presence of one of her countrymen, the shared shorthand that comes from being raised in the same place and seeing the world through the lens of the country that birthed you. It's pleasant talking to him, and after the nightmare, the urge to have memories of Cuba chase the shadows away is inescapable.

"What is Havana like now?" she asks him.

Julio hesitates. "Tense. On the precipice of change—you can feel it in the air, but what that change will amount to is anyone's guess. It's a volatile time to be in the city, with so many interests at play. It can be dangerous. There are a lot of people looking for revenge there, too. It's only been a year since the revolution, and they're still hunting Machado's supporters. And then there are those who are against Batista and the regime he has ushered in. There is a great deal of trouble in Havana now. But it's worth it. I wouldn't want to be anywhere else in the world."

Silence falls between them, the emotions inside her bubbling uncomfortably close to the surface.

"Do you want to dance?" Julio asks.

Surprise fills her as she glances around the deck space. It is empty enough this evening, everyone else either asleep or driven inside to dance with the band, but still—

"Right here? Right now?"

"Seems as good a place as any."

She hesitates. "Why?"

"Why not? You look like you want to dance even if you don't want to join in with their dancing, for which I can't blame you."

"I'm hardly dressed for a formal ball."

"You look nice enough to me."

She laughs at his decidedly unromantic delivery. "On that note, how can I resist."

He settles his hand on her waist lightly and takes her hand with his free one.

It's been ages since she danced, but it comes back to her easily, and there's something fun about taking this moment for herself and doing something so out of character, in engaging in an activity she once loved.

He's a lively dancer, more enthusiasm than practiced skill, and she imagines that their experiences were honed in far different places—his in low-lit bars and belowdecks, whereas hers came from the formal parties she attended with her family when she was a young girl in Vedado.

When the song switches to another, they both continue dancing without speaking, some mutual agreement in their bodies to carry on despite the beginnings of an ache in her calves. The more she dances, the more she can feel the nervous energy from the nightmare pouring out of her. When she was in the city and she would have bad dreams, she would go out on the street and walk for hours, reviewing the plan in her mind until exhaustion overtook her, sleep finally bringing peace. Tonight, dancing will do the trick.

Suddenly, the band stops playing, and another burst of laughter from the guests escapes the ballroom, tugging her out of the distraction the dancing has brought and placing her right back on the deck, all her problems still present and bearing down her neck.

"I should return to my cabin. It's late. Thank you for the dance, though. You were right; it was exactly what I needed."

"I'm glad," he replies. "I should go, too."

Elena smiles and walks on, heading back toward her cabin.

"Wait," Julio calls after her when she's only a few steps away. She stops, turning to face him.

"If you are in danger, if the revenge you seek becomes too much trouble, you can call on me for assistance," he says.

"Why would you insert yourself into someone else's troubles? You don't even know me; I could be anyone. You saw what I took out of that crate. I could be a murderer."

"Maybe. I've no doubt you're willing to do whatever you must to get what you want. Nor do I doubt you're capable of it. You'd be surprised how many people are when their existence is threatened. But I also know what fear looks like, and for all you talk about wanting to avenge the wrong that has been done to you, you're clearly afraid. I wouldn't be much of a gentleman if I didn't volunteer my help if it was needed."

She considers his offer for a moment. After the scene on the deck earlier, she'd be foolish not to. Her plan is a dangerous one, and he's the sort of man who likely knows his way around precarious situations if he is smuggling weapons to Cuba.

Still, it's difficult to know whom you can trust when you have been betrayed such as she has.

The truth—the whole of it, at least—is out of the question, but he knows she is a friend of Miguel's and saw her with the gun, so at this point he's already somewhat involved. Perhaps she has some use for him after all.

Elena takes a deep breath. "There is one thing you could do for me."

CHAPTER SIX

CATHERINE

Our second day on the *Morro Castle* passes much like the first. We're at sea, on our long journey from New York to Havana, and the crew seems determined to keep us busy with games, entertainments, and frivolities. There's a mock horse race going on, the cruise director cheering for the guests as everyone places their wager for which "horse" will win.

From the moment I wake, I'm filled with nerves, waiting to see if there will be an announcement about a missing guest, if the absence of the man who attacked me last night has been noted, but so far there is nothing, and when we dine at breakfast, the conversation is centered on everyone's plans for the day rather than the news that someone went overboard last night.

Why has no one noticed that he is missing?

I wrack my brain throughout the meal, giving little attention to the omelet before me, trying to place him among the guests whose paths I crossed since we boarded the *Morro Castle*, but I cannot remember seeing him on the sundeck or at dinner. There are a fair number of single travelers on the cruise who have come to meet others and it's possible that he came alone as well, but I keep thinking someone—if not another one of the passengers, then one of the crew, his stateroom attendant, perhaps—will discover his absence and raise the alarm.

I considered asking around, using the name Harry found on his identification in his wallet, but if he does turn up missing later, the last thing I need is for people to remember that I was inquiring about him.

After the two of us have breakfast together, Raymond leaves me alone once more. I head to Ava's room to see how she and Emily are faring on the voyage. As far as I know, Raymond has yet to visit his daughter since we boarded the *Morro Castle*, and while the girl's nanny seems competent and professional enough, she is a recent addition to the household, and I can't help but feel bad for the child. It must be difficult to spend so much time in the company of a near stranger.

Ava seems content enough when I visit their stateroom, although truthfully, I have little experience with children. She's an agreeable enough child, which I suppose comes with the territory of being raised by a series of nannies and an uninvolved parent. While I like to think she is comfortable with me, the truth is that as much as I worry for her, I find myself awkwardly trying to bond with her, lacking the right words and mannerisms to engage a toddler. No doubt I'm a poor substitute for her mother, domestic life hardly coming naturally to me.

I had wondered—and worried—how this cruise would go, if Raymond would expect this to be a precursor to our married life and for us to spend as much time together as possible. Courtship is so much easier to conduct when you see little of each other, your interactions confined to carefully selected activities and curated impressions. Intimacy is another matter entirely. The key to hooking Raymond was to preserve an air of mystery about myself while also laying the groundwork with just enough clues to give him the impression that I am who I pretend to be. If we lived in each other's pockets all cruise, I think the illusion would wear off rather quickly.

After visiting with Ava and her nanny Emily, I lie on deck for nearly the whole day, contenting myself with my novel and the sun and sea air. It's impossible to keep from scanning the deck for Harry, too, considering our newfound secret, but wherever he is, our paths have not yet crossed.

As the sunlight recedes, the sun setting, I am loath to leave the comfort of the lounge chair for tonight's dinner, when I will be forced to don the mask I wear once more.

There's something freeing about being out at sea, as though the normal social niceties have been erased and we can all relax a bit with less concern for what others think of us or the impression we make. However, in the dining room, the atmosphere is such that we might as well be in New York again—the formality and pomp suffocating. But here on the deck, with little more than the ocean and the horizon in front of me, I imagine that I could disappear from this life I have crafted for myself and just be Katie once more.

I read far longer than I should, and it hardly registers that the deck is clearing out of guests preparing for the evening festivities. There's barely time for me to bathe and dress for dinner before I'm due to meet Raymond.

I take less care with my appearance than I normally would, eager to hopefully squeeze in a few minutes and another chapter or two before dinner. If things were different, I'd happily forgo the meal altogether and curl up in bed with my novel.

I manage several more pages before dinner, Raymond waiting for me near the entrance of the grand ballroom. I fancifully considered slipping the book into my evening bag for a tantalizing moment and trying to sneak a chapter in at the table.

Raymond looks to be in relatively good spirits, thankfully. Much of my time is spent analyzing his moods, trying to unwrap the riddle that is my fiancé. Part of ensnaring him was learning to make myself pleasing to him so that I echoed his likes, soothed his worries, smoothed over his bad-tempered moments. It's a delicate dance, and one I normally excel at, although tonight my heart isn't in it.

I don't want to be here, don't want to spend my evening pretending to be someone I'm not.

We dine with the same partners from the first evening minus a few who are missing—including Harry—the conversation not much different than it was at the captain's table. Tonight, there are new guests in our place being regaled by stories of grand sea adventures. I can't help but peruse the room for a sign of Harry, but he's nowhere to be seen.

The band is quite good tonight, the mood lively, Raymond even choosing to take a turn around the ballroom with me after dinner. He's a capable dancer like so many of his ilk are.

The song changes from a familiar hit I recognize to a melody I don't, the words in Spanish no doubt a nod to our impending disembarkation in Havana.

Suddenly, Raymond trips, the motion sending me lurching backward, throwing out my arms to steady myself and keep from falling to the ground. Curious glances are cast our way, but it's not their reaction that stands out to me most.

It's my fiancé's.

Raymond's face has gone pale.

"Is everything alright?" I ask once I have righted myself from my awkward stumble.

He doesn't answer me.

"Raymond?"

"Yes. I just—this song—"

He doesn't finish his thought or seem to think he must explain his behavior, because the next thing I know he takes my hand, hurrying me out of the ballroom and heading toward the open deck outside.

He stops when we near the railing, and belatedly I realize that we are auspiciously close to the place where the man went overboard. I take a step back from the railing and then another, visions of *my* body toppling into the ocean filling me.

Raymond stares out at the water, his hands braced on the railing, his mouth set in a thin line.

"Is everything alright?" I ask again.

"Yes, of course," he replies, turning his attention back to me.

"Did that song upset you? I confess I don't think I've ever seen you so ruffled," I add, careful to keep my voice light. In the six months since we started dating, I've learned that Raymond does not like to be questioned, particularly by women.

"No, of course not," he lies, despite the obvious evidence to the contrary.

Are all wealthy men like this—treating the women in their lives as though they're obtuse to avoid having conversations they do not wish to have? And is it supposed to be my society-imposed womanly duty to reassure him that I believe him beyond all reason and logic?

"I've never heard that particular song before," I muse, unable to resist exploring his reaction further. "It's quite beautiful. You seemed to know it well."

"No, not well," he replies, his expression cross, although whether his ire is directed at me or the song, I'll never know. "I've only heard it once before. At a wedding. I didn't think many people knew it."

"Whose wedding?" I ask, surprised by his uncharacteristic forthrightness, although I almost get the impression that he is speaking aloud to himself, working something out in his mind rather than sharing details with me.

"No one important."

I open my mouth to respond, when he reaches out, putting his hands on my waist.

A spark of fear fills me, the memory of last night with the strange man on the deck crashing back into me once more. A scream builds in my throat.

Raymond leans forward and smashes his mouth against mine.

I freeze, momentarily caught between fight or flight, my body here in the now and somehow my mind caught in the past, when that man attacked me.

Raymond's kiss feels like an invasion of sorts. I reach up, grasping his arms, ready to push him away, but his grip on me is ironclad, and slowly my mind comes back to me, and I remember where I am, that I am with my fiancé, that the danger I sensed a moment ago is gone.

I let him kiss me.

Raymond kisses like the sort of man who knows how to kiss but doesn't particularly care if you enjoy it or not. There's nothing wrong with his kisses, they're perfectly *fine* in a physical sense, but it's the difference between an artist with technical proficiency and little passion and one who creates from their heart.

In the beginning, his kisses were softer, pliant, as though he was attempting to seduce me each time he held me in his arms. Now that we are engaged, he kisses me with expectation, as if this is little more than a precursor to the main event. Each time, I worry more and more that he will push me to take things further than I am comfortable, that he wants more from me than I am willing to give.

It's over as quickly as it began, and Raymond releases me.

My heart pounds, and I take a deep breath, dragging the air back into my lungs. My gaze drifts over the deck—

Harry stands near one of the ship's doors, watching us, his expression inscrutable.

There's a woman a few steps back, watching him, watching *all* of us, but she turns before I can make out her face, until all I can see is a flash of dark hair and a somber navy dress.

When I return to my stateroom after the evening's festivities, a note waits for me on the bed, my name scribbled on the outside in unfamiliar handwriting.

Meet me on deck at midnight. You know where.

There's nothing necessarily threatening in the words, but

the *'you know where'* gives me pause. The only significant place on the *Morro Castle* that I can think of is the deck where I was last evening and earlier with Raymond. But does that mean that someone saw Harry and me together last night when we dumped the man's body overboard, or am I merely worrying for nothing? And then as I read the words again, trying to decipher any clues from the handwriting, I can't help but wonder:

Did Harry leave this note for me?

I imagine he has all sorts of skill with entering guests' staterooms, considering his line of work.

According to the clock in my cabin, it's already an hour past midnight, the evening going longer than I intended, so whoever did want to meet me is likely gone by now. But then I remember Harry standing on the deck watching the kiss between me and Raymond. Was that around midnight? Was he waiting for me? Did he think I had returned to my cabin and had a chance to see this missive? Was he expecting to find me there alone?

I tear the paper into little pieces, throwing them in the wastebasket, lest anyone find them. It's the sort of note that implies an indiscretion, and the last thing I need is for Raymond to find it and become suspicious.

I sit on the edge of the bed, reaching down to unbuckle my sandals.

If it was Harry, maybe he's heard something about the missing man that he wants to share with me.

I leave my stateroom and head for the open deck.

Harry stands at the railing near where we tossed the man overboard, his hands shoved in his pockets and his gaze cast out to the sea.

As I walk toward him, the sound of my footsteps echoing across the deck, he turns slowly.

"Returning to the scene of the crime?" His voice is low enough against the backdrop of the roaring wind for his words to be for me alone.

"I should ask you the same thing," I reply. "You were here first."

"I lost a cuff link. I didn't realize it until this evening when my valet said something. I thought perhaps in the struggle to lift his body—"

Oh no.

"Did you find it?"

"No. It must have gone overboard. Or perhaps when the crew cleaned the deck, they swept it up."

"Were the cuff links monogrammed?"

He shoots me a look. "Do I look like the sort of man who has monogrammed cuff links? They're rather a hindrance given my career interests. Don't fret; they're perfectly ordinary cuff links. If anyone finds them, they'll hardly think anything suspicious."

"But what if they connect them to you? What if someone found it, what if—"

"Relax. Even if they did find it, there's a plausible explanation to be had. It doesn't mean anything more than an inconvenience."

It's weirdly calming to see how unruffled he is by the entire business, but then again, that probably comes with the territory.

Harry leans back against the railing, studying me. "So, if you didn't come out here to revisit last night, what brought you out here so intently and without the company of your charming fiancé, no less? Please tell me you came to find me because you've realized you're engaged to a dreadful bore, and you've decided you'd rather have some fun instead."

"Raymond is not a bore," I bluff.

"I played cards with the man earlier today. I'd beg to differ. He is a *bore*. Easy enough to read, as well."

"Raymond doesn't play cards."

He chuckles. "Is that what he told you? Let me guess, he's too virtuous to gamble?"

"Something like that."

"He's in finance, isn't he? Investment? What is that if not a big gamble, particularly in these uncertain times."

"That's different," I reply, even though I can't deny he has a point.

Harry sighs as though he's bored with me and this entire conversation. "Well, I hate to shatter the illusion, but your

Raymond plays a great deal of cards. At least, he has done so since we boarded the *Morro Castle*."

So that's where he's been while I've been on deck reading.

"What sort of gambler is he?" I ask.

"Not a very good one based on the money he's lost. Although I suppose he must have very deep pockets to lose as much and as often as he does."

"He does have very deep pockets."

"A match made in heaven. I imagine those pockets of his are very important, considering you're not in love."

"Of course I am. I wouldn't be getting married if I wasn't in love," I lie.

"Please. We both know there are plenty of reasons to marry, and love certainly isn't a prerequisite."

"Well, it is for me."

"You were kissing him with your eyes wide open on the deck. You hardly looked like you were in the throes of passion. More like you were bored."

"You shouldn't have been watching us. And I wasn't bored, but it was weird being back here after what happened last night. I kept remembering the moment when the man attacked me— when his body went over the water."

"I haven't heard anything about a missing guest if you're concerned about that."

"I haven't heard anything, either. That seems strange, right? Surely, someone would miss a guest who goes overboard this early in the cruise. I mean, at the end of the cruise it's probably easy enough to disappear and have people assume you disembarked and were missed in the crush, but surely someone will notice his stateroom is abandoned, or that—"

"You'd be surprised. There are always unoccupied cabins on the ship. Sometimes a bribe is all it takes for someone to avoid being on the official manifest and stay in one of those. It's far more common than you realize."

"I wish there were a way to ask about him, to find out if he was officially listed as a guest, without anyone realizing it."

"I wouldn't recommend it. People will remember you asking about him and that's the last thing we need."

I sigh. "I know. I came to the same conclusion earlier. I just hate feeling helpless, as though I am waiting for the other shoe to drop."

He frowns. "Are you alright? I know the man has you worried, but you were a lot calmer last night. You seemed—unsettled when I saw you earlier. Has something else happened?"

Embarrassment fills me. The last thing I want is for him to think I'm some sort of damsel in distress in need of rescuing. I've been taking care of myself my entire life and I have no desire for that to change now. Besides, he's hardly a trustworthy partner.

"I'm surprised to find you out here," I say, ignoring his question.

"Why? There's only so much you can do on a ship in the middle of the ocean. Especially when the novelty of the itinerary has worn off after so many voyages. I can only play so many cards before my hand starts to cramp and the thrill of divesting our fellow passengers of their ill-gotten gains fades."

"It's a veritable den of iniquity with the drinking, and the gambling, and everything else. There's no shortage of trouble to get into on a ship like this. I would think it would be exactly what you're looking for."

"Trust me, it all tends to run together after a while. It's hard to find excitement when the outrageous becomes the banal."

"What a struggle it must be for you, leading a life of such decadence."

He laughs. "You'd be surprised. So, what's *your* game?"

"Don't leave me any more notes," I say, ignoring his question once more.

"I didn't send you a note."

"There was a note on my pillow asking me to meet you on the deck at midnight. I didn't see it until I returned to my cabin, and it was already too late."

"If there was, it wasn't from me."

He doesn't seem like he's lying, and he hardly appears to care about his reputation overly much. But if he didn't send me the note, who did?

"I thought it was you—that perhaps it was about what happened last night. It referenced something about how I would know where to meet, like it was a place that was significant for me, and this is the only location that qualifies on the *Morro Castle*. I thought maybe you had heard something about the man who attacked me." I feel silly now for jumping to conclusions, for dashing off without considering that maybe the note was dangerous. Was someone attempting to blackmail me or trying to get me alone on the ship?

"If no one is looking for him, count yourself lucky. The last thing you need is the authorities getting involved. There are all sorts of people on this ship; some with purer motives than others, some with more disreputable reputations than others. Maybe the reason no one has reported his absence is that he was here with nefarious purposes in mind; it certainly bodes with his behavior toward you on the ship."

"Why don't you go that route?"

"What—smuggle myself on board or slip someone money to keep my name off the records?"

I nod.

"Where's the fun in that? Besides, my job is infinitely easier when I can get close to my marks, when I can examine the jewelry with a practiced eye and see if what they have is worth stealing. You'd be surprised how often you think something is valuable only to later realize on closer inspection that it's worth nothing at all. Besides, it gives me a chance to know the people I'm stealing from, to get a sense of them. Believe it or not, I take care in the people whose jewelry I lift. After all, I know what it's like to have nothing—I'd never take something that was irreplaceable to someone who needed it."

I'm not sure what to make of his explanation, nor do I know why it matters whether I believe his words or not. I understand better than anyone how easy it is to rationalize one's actions, and maybe that's all he's doing, selling himself a story that enables him to live with the consequences of his decisions.

"Have you made any other friends on this voyage?" Harry asks. "Perhaps one of them left you a note."

"I would hardly call us friends, and as a matter of fact, no, I haven't had much time to make the acquaintance of the other passengers."

"You've certainly missed out, then. Some of them have fascinating—"

"—Jewelry collections?" I finish.

He flashes me a wolfish grin. "Indeed they do. I don't know what to tell you, but it wasn't from me. Maybe it was meant for someone else, and they had the wrong cabin."

I try to remember the words written on the paper, my fear over Raymond finding it keeping me from poring over the message as carefully as I would have liked. Certainly, there must be a fair share of romantic trysts going on.

"Perhaps."

His gaze narrows slightly. "Are you concerned?"

"The wording was innocuous enough. But—"

"Given the fact that a man attacked you on the deck last night, maybe you should be more concerned."

I'll check the wastebasket for the note when I return to my stateroom. Is Harry right—should I be looking over my shoulder?

"Not that I mind seeing you again," Harry adds. "Although

we really should stop making a habit of this considering you're an engaged woman. But then again, I think there's a part of you that likes it."

I ignore his last words, my mind picking apart the events of the last few days.

"What do you know about this cruise?" I ask him.

"What do you mean?"

"You said you've been on the *Morro Castle* quite a few times. Have you ever known it to be dangerous?"

"I suppose that depends on what you mean by 'dangerous.' There are lots of rumors surrounding the ship—that weapons are being smuggled to Cuba, people being rescued from Cuba. There are others like me working the cruise—thieves and con artists alike. So, I suppose in a way, yes, it is dangerous depending on who you are and whose interest you've piqued. Plenty of people come here for a weeklong vacation, but others have more nefarious purposes. It's not much different than life, really."

I've been so focused on myself, that I've not been paying enough attention clearly. I won't make the same mistake again.

"I should go back to my cabin. It's getting late."

"It's not that late. You could stay out here and look at the stars."

"Is that a line?"

"No, it isn't. Honestly, you look tired, and you seem as though you have a million thoughts running through your head. I do my best work when I can clear my mind a bit. When I can relax. It's not good to worry all the time. You find yourself focusing on the wrong things and missing the obvious ones. You look like hell. You look like you need a break."

He closes the distance between us and reaches out, lightly caressing my cheek, his fingers stroking my earlobe.

He does, indeed, have magic hands.

"Let go, Catherine. Just for a moment," he whispers.

He releases me as quickly as he caressed me, a question in the pause, and then his hands drift from the curve of my cheek to my waist. I allow him to gently turn me to face the water. Earlier, when I was this close to the sea and the railing with Raymond, I felt a sense of fear, the vision of me tumbling overboard assailing me.

Now, different sensations fill me as I brace my hands against the railing and stare out at the ocean, Harry standing behind me, his hands coming to rest on either side of mine, bracketing me, his body shielding me from the view of any onlookers.

It's dangerous standing with a man in public like this, even if it is late enough that the deck is empty for now. Harry doesn't lean into me, but still, I'm aware of how close we are to each other.

We stare out at the water, not speaking, a whisper between us.

It isn't until an hour later—when I'm undressing in my stateroom, and I study my reflection in the mirror—that I realize the emerald earrings Raymond gifted to me are gone.

CHAPTER SEVEN

ELENA

Elena tugs on the maid's outfit she borrowed from the crew's storeroom earlier, the uniform slightly too small for her frame, but not so obviously that it would draw suspicion from anyone who saw her in the first-class corridor.

Her gaze darts around the hallway. It's past midnight, but many of the guests are out on deck enjoying the evening weather and starry skies, others ensconced in sitting rooms around the ship playing cards until the wee hours of the morning.

She raps on the door once, twice for good measure.

"I've come to clean your stateroom. Is this a convenient time?" she calls out to be sure the room is indeed empty as she planned.

No one answers from the other side of the door.

She glances to the side, but there's no one there. Worst case, if anyone is questioned about this later, hopefully all they'll remember is seeing one of the maids go in to clean the state-rooms. No matter that their usual evening rotation is hours earlier. The passengers can be demanding, the crew accommodating all sorts of odd requests at all times of day, the guests maintaining their own erratic schedules.

The key she filched from the storeroom slides into the lock easily, and she opens the door quickly, carefully checking the seam of the door for any booby traps he may have left along the way, a string that he will be able to tell is broken when he returns or something similar.

She underestimated what he was capable of once. It's a mistake that won't happen again.

There's nothing. The door is clear.

It's almost insulting to think that for as focused as she has been on him, he's completely unaware of the danger lurking just a few decks down from him.

Fine.

It's better that way. That when she strikes, he least expects it.

It was risky to ask the roving waiter to have the band play their wedding song earlier, but seeing him dancing like that—

Watching him with another woman was surprisingly less painful than she imagined it would be, but still, the desire to see if he would remember, to compel him to think of her while she lurked in the shadows, was too great to ignore.

Elena closes the door behind her gently, scanning the room for any last-minute signs of life, an excuse on the tip of her tongue until even that falls away.

For a moment, she can't move, her body frozen to the spot near the front door, the sights and smells of the room sending a chill down her spine. She reaches behind her, gripping the doorknob for purchase, to keep her knees from buckling beneath her and to prevent her body from sinking to the floor.

Memories flood her, one by one.

His cologne is unchanged, the familiar scent conjuring her past. One of his shirts is discarded over a chair in the stateroom and her fingers burn as she remembers rubbing the fabric between her fingers as her hands caressed his body. The sight of his personal effects reminds her of what it was like in the beginning, when she was so in love, when she believed that they had found happiness and that she would have nothing but safety in his arms.

She takes a deep breath and then another, pushing the thoughts from her mind and steeling herself for the task at hand. She should have realized this would happen, should have prepared better for it.

There's no room for weakness now.

When her nerves are steadied, Elena heads toward the dresser, opening the top drawer and sifting through Raymond's things.

She goes through the dresser quickly, careful to keep from

disturbing the natural order, to avoid creasing his well-pressed clothing. He was always the sort of man who noticed little about others, but a great deal about his possessions.

When the search through the dresser yields nothing of interest, she moves on, the urge to wreak havoc in this room overwhelming, the desire to shred and destroy his life as he has done to hers nearly overpowering the entire purpose of this visit.

Revenge has settled in her breast, and the need to see him brought to his knees is all that sustains her some days. It has never been in her nature to be patient and wait, to bank her emotions, to suffer in silence.

It takes ten minutes of searching for her to find what she's looking for—a stack of papers tucked away in a briefcase in the back of Raymond's closet. She could have waited a bit longer into the cruise, but she's never been one for leaving things to the last minute in case a plan goes awry, and everything hinges on her success tonight.

She scans the words carefully, poring over the documents as quickly as she can. There's a great deal of legal wording in the will, different accounts in the banking documents, some she recognizes and some she doesn't.

Her fingers tremble when she looks at the two documents that have played such a large role in her life—

Her marriage certificate and her death certificate.

Suddenly, she hears footsteps padding down the corridor outside Raymond's stateroom.

The papers slip out of her hand, fluttering to the ground.

"Damn," Elena hisses, bending down to pick them up when—

The sound of a key entering the lock—

She grabs the papers, holding them to her breast, her heart beating madly as her gaze darts around the room, searching for a hiding place.

The lock turns.

She dives under the bed, papers in hand, just as the sound of the door opening fills the room, followed by footsteps and then the door closing, the lock turning with a soft click.

Her breath seems unnaturally loud to her own ears as she lies on the floor beneath the bed, her belly pressed to the carpet, the documents clutched in her hand. The bed skirt covers most of the distance between the mattress and the ground save for a small sliver where the light from the room shines through, but it's hardly enough to see who has entered the room, if it's one of the maids or Raymond himself, returned to his room for the evening.

The sound of water running from a faucet fills the room.

Did she leave the bathroom door open like it was when she came in here or did she close it behind her? She was so careful when she went through the room, trying to memorize the way everything was to ensure that she returned it to the same condition to avoid arousing his suspicion. Now that she's trapped beneath the bed, though, she fears she made a mistake, that Raymond will realize someone has been in his room and begin looking for the perpetrator.

Of course, once he realizes the papers are gone, it'll all be over, but she hopes by that point it will be too late for him to do anything about it.

A drawer opens and then another, a hastily offered curse filling the cabin.

The sound of that voice sends a chill down her spine.

There's no question about it. It's Raymond.

What if he's turned in for the night? Will she really be stuck here until he falls asleep? Her neck aches, a crick forming from lying on her stomach.

For a moment, she considers just doing it now, crawling out from under the bed and confronting him since he's alone. But as quickly as the thought enters her mind, the impulse tantalizing in the immediate gratification it would bring, it escapes, because the reality is that he can overpower her quickly, and in this room where there's no one to bear witness to his perfidy, it would be the easiest thing in the world for him to do away with her once and for all and simply hide the body or toss it overboard.

Minutes pass with Raymond puttering around the room. Elena holds her breath, sure that at some moment he will notice her breathing and look under the bed. She strains to hear if he is removing his clothing to prepare for sleep, but instead *finally, finally* the door to the stateroom closes with a click.

She waits a few minutes in her hiding place to make sure that he doesn't return and then crawls out from under the bed, the legal documents in her hand.

She glances down at them quickly once more to make sure that they are indeed what she came for, the wording of the will bringing a smile to her lips.

This won't right the wrong Raymond did to her—not entirely—but it certainly will help.

Elena closes the door to the stateroom behind her, and then she's gone, just another unseen member of the housekeeping staff moving through the ship's corridors, a fortune in her hands.

CHAPTER EIGHT

CATHERINE

"Give them back," I demand, closing the door to Harry's cabin behind me, turning the lock with a decisive click.

I didn't bother dressing, my robe tied tightly around my waist. Given the late hour, the hallways were empty, his room only a few doors down from mine.

At this rate, I'll oversleep for breakfast, but I can't find it in me to care. I cannot believe he had the audacity to steal my earrings after that business with Mrs. Gregory's bracelet.

"You're beginning to look awfully comfortable in my stateroom." Harry grins, leaning back in his chair, his ankles crossed over each other. "What are you talking about? Give what back? I haven't the faintest. Not that I'm complaining if it brings you back here."

I cross the distance between us in a few strides. "The earrings you took earlier. Give them back. Now."

His smile widens, his gaze raking over my state of dishabille. "If I'd known you were so desperate to see me again, I happily would have invited you to my cabin. Why, we could have even had a nightcap together." He rises from his seat so smoothly, so quickly that I don't realize he's come so close until I can feel his breath on my bare skin, can smell his cologne and a faint hint of the starch his valet must use to press his dress shirts. He's dressed for bed, too, the elegant silk dressing gown that I saw draped over the chair in his room the last time I was here wrapped around his lithe body.

"I don't want to have a nightcap with you, and believe me, your cabin is the last place I want to be. But my fiancé gave me those earrings, and if I'm not wearing them tomorrow, he'll be very disappointed."

"I imagine he'd be even more disappointed if he learned *how* you lost them," Harry murmurs, his voice suddenly gone husky. He raises his hand, and a tremor slides down my spine as his fingers stroke my neck leaving a trail of goose bumps in their wake. "I enjoyed our time on the deck together."

"You're good with your hands, I'll give you that," I reply, my voice tart.

He chuckles. "I'm *very* good with my hands in more ways than one. Aren't you just a little bit curious to see how good I can be?"

"Not even a bit," I huff, even as I lean toward him, enjoying the sensation far too much, the electricity crackling between us coursing through me.

One of the drawbacks of pretending to be a proper lady is that you must *act* like a proper lady, and everyone knows they have absolutely no fun at all.

The knowing gleam in Harry's eyes makes me think he's aware of my predicament.

"The earrings." I hold out my hand impatiently.

"Has anyone ever told you that you look positively imperious when you do that?"

If he only knew how much time I had spent in front of my mirror testing out that very look before launching it in society. Although, given the twitch of his lips, I'm beginning to think he suspects it.

"The earrings," I demand once again.

He smiles, and suddenly, the late hour hits me, the sheer *inconvenience* of this entire business flooding me. I have no time for a man like this, no time for seduction, or playful indiscretions. I have no time for the way that I feel. Not with so much at stake.

"What's your end game here? Do you think to steal me away from my fiancé?"

He laughs, the sound full and rich. "I couldn't afford you if I wanted to."

"Then why do you take such delight in tormenting me?"

"Tormenting you? I helped you, remember? Last night and

then again this evening when you looked lost in the moon-light."

I bristle at his words, at the romanticism in them, and the portrait he paints of me as some sort of wounded bird.

"I thought we agreed that you would dispense with the terrible lines. They don't work on me, and honestly, if I were you, I'd be more than a little embarrassed to be using them."

"What would work on you?"

"I have no idea. Not much."

"Let me ask you a question, then," he continues. "From one friend to another. When did Raymond give you the earrings?"

"How is that any of your business?"

"Call it curiosity."

"Before we boarded the ship. They were a birthday present. Raymond enjoys being generous."

"He's not generous. They're fake."

"Don't be ridiculous. Of course they aren't fake. They were in a jewelry box from Cartier when he gave them to me."

I've already mentally calculated the price they'll fetch if this whole thing goes south, and I figure this gift alone will set me up nicely.

"He may have put them in a jewelry box, but those earrings are no more from Cartier than I am. They're glass. Not even a particularly good fake, to be honest. From a distance, they pass muster well enough, but get them under a loupe and well . . . bubbles. Everywhere. I've dealt in fakes a time or two in my day, and you can get some good ones, but these aren't it."

"I don't believe you."

"Suit yourself. Take them to a jeweler when you get to New York or in Havana and see what they say. I know jewelry, and anyone else who does, too, will recognize they're fake."

He reaches into his pocket and wordlessly pulls a jeweler's loupe from his pocket.

"I see you're not even trying to pretend you're respectable."

"I could be a respectable jeweler."

"But you're not."

"Of course not."

He hands the loupe to me.

Our fingers brush against each other when I take it from him.

"Raymond is one of the wealthiest men in New York City. He must have made a mistake buying them or he must have been swindled by the person he bought them from, but there's no way he would have given me fake stones. For what purpose? You're wrong."

"I'm not, and that's a good question—one you should be asking yourself."

There's nothing in Harry's demeanor and expression that suggests he's lying, but his claims just don't add up. I've seen how wealthy Raymond is; it's impossible to miss it. Rich men don't buy their fiancées fake jewels.

"Real or not, I *need* them back. Or would you prefer I go to the police and let them know to search your cabin?"

"You wound me. I'll give them back if you ask nicely. And if you go to the police, then I suppose I'll have to do the same and tell them how I watched you toss a man overboard."

"If you incriminate me, you're implicating yourself as well. I don't think anyone would believe I lifted that body all by myself."

"Maybe, maybe not. But if you aren't the heiress you're pretending to be, then I have a feeling you don't want the police digging into your past. People who shroud themselves in lies tend to have a skeleton or two in their closet."

"Bastard."

"That is regrettably true, but then again, I've never cared all that much for propriety."

Regret instantly fills me.

"I didn't mean it literally—not like that—believe me, I am the last person to judge someone for the circumstances of their birth. My origins certainly aren't auspicious."

"It's fine. It's not the first time I've heard it and I doubt it will be the last. My father wasn't the sort of man I would want to claim me anyway."

"What sort of man was your father?"

"A rich one. Married, too. Not to my mother, of course. She was a seamstress, and his wife was one of her clients. He was a British lord with a minor, unimportant, decaying title who came to America to find a rich wife. Once he wed her, he set out having as much fun as he could."

"*He* sounds like a bastard."

"He was. He was also a man who always got what he wanted and didn't take no for an answer. My mother was very young and very beautiful. When she went to their home to deliver his wife's gowns, as soon as he saw her, he decided he wanted her even if she didn't want him. He pressed his advances quite ardently, to hear my mother tell it, threatened to spread stories about her being promiscuous to drive away the wealthy, powerful clients who could afford her dresses if she didn't give in."

I reach out and lay a hand on his arm. "Harry, I'm so sorry. I shouldn't have asked."

The world he describes is all too familiar to me as someone who grew up serving others, living her life precariously, afraid that one wrong move, one dismissal could lead to ruination. I know all about men who believe the world is theirs for the taking and are willing to do anything to satisfy their needs and desires.

"No, it's alright that you did. The shame is his, not mine. My mother—my mother bore it, though. He left her when he learned she was pregnant, her body no longer of any use to him. He gave her enough to barely feed us for a couple years and then abdicated all responsibility, went back to his rich wife and probably another young seamstress, or maid, or cook he could force himself on."

"I'm sorry."

"Be careful, Catherine. There's something about Raymond— a disregard for others, disdain for anyone he views as beneath him. He reminds me of my father, of all those men of his ilk. Whatever your game is, don't think he doesn't have one of his own."

"What happened with your father?"

"I killed him."

Shock fills me. "You—"

"He took me hunting when I turned eighteen. He hadn't any sons, only daughters, you see, and suddenly, at the end of his life, his blasted title in jeopardy, he remembered the bastard son he fathered and thought I might be his way of carrying on the family lineage. It's such a pathetic cliché, but his legacy was everything to him as it is with so many men with an over-inflated sense of their own importance.

"My mother had just died. She often struggled with her health, and we didn't have enough money for doctors, didn't have enough money for anything, really. She had lived with the same shame my entire life, carried the horror of what that man did to her. That day that we went hunting, all I could think of was my mother's eyes and the pain that would cross her face when she looked at me, when she saw flashes of him in my appearance. It didn't feel right that she wasn't avenged—that he was never made to take responsibility for his actions, that because he was powerful and wealthy thanks to his marriage, he never would be accountable no matter how many women he violated. So, I shot him."

Harry says it without any remorse, his expression fairly goading me to react, to condemn him.

Instead, I take a step forward and wrap my arms around him.

He doesn't move, his body gone rigid, and I wonder at the last time anyone showed him comfort. I've no doubt he's had pleasure in spades considering the way women watch him, but the simple act of someone hugging him seems to throw him for a loop.

Truthfully, I can't remember the last time I gave someone comfort, either.

We both stand there awkwardly, two people occupying roles we're wholly unused to, our hard edges momentarily sanded down.

"I would have done the same thing," I whisper, trying to give him solace, to let him know that for all we've sparred, for all I've given him a hard time for stealing, I understand.

"Would you?" he asks, pulling back slightly, studying my face. He nods at whatever he sees there. "Yes, I imagine you would."

"How did you avoid getting caught?"

"I was terrified after it happened. I hadn't planned on killing him. I said it was an accident. I was an inexperienced hunter, that sort of thing happens. The rich wife hated my father nearly as much as I did, and now that she was a widow, she gained a freedom she didn't have when he married her for her money. She was aware of his plans to claim me, and knowing that doing so would have entitled me to *her* money, well, let's just say I had rid her of a problem, too. She paid me in exchange for the promise that I would disappear from their lives forever. One I happily made, and the money was an excellent chance for me to reinvent myself."

"Did it help?"

I don't finish the thought, but he knows what I mean because he answers, "No. I thought it would. Maybe I was foolish to think that. Some things always stick with you no matter what. I'd like to believe I've moved on, that his ghost doesn't haunt me anymore, but I don't know how true that is. His blood is in me whether I like it or not."

"That doesn't mean you're his son, that you're anything like him."

Harry is the first one to move, the hands wrapped around my back stroking now, tracing the line of my spine through my robe, caressing my waist, moving higher, higher still.

I know he's going to kiss me before his mouth meets mine, know I am going to kiss him back before our lips touch and everything changes.

It's unlike anything I've ever experienced, his lips plundering mine, and from the first moment, I meet him kiss for kiss, vying for control, sucking his bottom lip into my mouth, nipping at the sensitive skin there until a low chuckle reverberates from him as his hands tighten around my waist. I refuse to *be kissed*, to be a passive participant in this, to allow him to take the lead, to have this moment be something that happens to me rather than something I choose for myself.

My hands fist his hair, tugging him closer to me, a moan of protest escaping my mouth when he abandons my lips, kissing his way down my throat, leaving a trail of goose bumps behind him, and then moving lower still to the open expanse of skin displayed by my robe.

I arch my back into his caress, the sensation of his lips on my skin nearly too much to bear. God help me, I want more of this, but even as the sensations overwhelm me, I pull back, the reality of what has just happened slamming into me as I struggle to calm my racing heart.

I can't afford to lose control.

Harry releases me instantly, taking a step back and then another, and if I am to be mollified by anything, it is the fact that he doesn't look much happier about this entire business than I do.

"We shouldn't have—"

"—No, we probably shouldn't," he agrees. "Flirtations aside, I don't need complications on this cruise, and you are undoubtedly a complication."

I open my mouth to argue with him, to point out the fact that he has been the one showing up all this time, teasing me, that I have hardly sought him out, that if anything I have been doing everything in my power to avoid a situation like this. But the words simply do not come, and I'm left staring at him, belatedly realizing that his hair is disheveled from my hands tugging at it, his lips swollen from the intensity of my kisses; is that a bite mark on his neck?

My cheeks heat as I remember nipping at his skin.

Harry says nothing, his gaze intent on me.

I must get out of here.

My voice shakes, embarrassment filling me at the way my body trembles as though it could ignite with just one touch.

"I need my earrings back. Really. Fake or not, Raymond will notice if I'm not wearing them."

Harry's eyes darken slightly as my fiancé's name falls from my lips.

"I don't know what you're talking about," he drawls. "You're wearing the same earrings you had on earlier."

I refuse to look away from him, to let him see me flinch as I raise my hand, my fingers trembling as they brush against the cold emerald stones now dangling from my ears once more.

It isn't until later when I'm back in the comfort of my stateroom that I look down at my hand and realize my engagement ring is gone.

CHAPTER NINE

After that kiss, well, it's little surprise that I barely slept, finally waking after a dream of me and Harry in his stateroom that was entirely too erotic for comfort. When I did wake, I realized I had overslept, missing breakfast with Raymond on our sea day. I sent a note with one of the crew to let Raymond know that I was sorry, that I hadn't been feeling well. *A feminine indisposition*, I wrote, knowing full well that any such mention would send a man running for the hills.

For the first few minutes when I woke up, I almost forgot everything that had happened, my mind blissfully blank. But then, little by little, it all came back to me, the bare space on my finger where my engagement ring should be taunting me.

Now that I know the folly and consequences of confronting Harry alone in his cabin, I'll have to be more cautious about how I get my ring back this time. I don't think I can face another kiss.

When I feel rested enough, I head to the first-class lounge with my book in hand for some light refreshments, my stomach growling after the missed breakfast. For all that Raymond suggested we take this cruise together to celebrate our impending marriage, we've spent little time together onboard the *Morro Castle* save for the social occasions like dinner, when it would be noticeable for me not to accompany him. Of Ava, I have seen even less. I've experienced enough of wealthy families to know this is more the norm than not, but it still feels strange to me in principle.

The first-class lounge is busy this afternoon, many guests clearly suffering the effects of a late evening the previous night. But then again, that's the appeal of a cruise such as this one—it takes you away from the drudgeries of schedules and wake-up times, responsibilities like work and home. I wonder how the crew feels watching us relax like this while they toil to keep the ship running. Perhaps in these economic times they are simply happy to have jobs, although I can't help but feel as though we are two extreme realities juxtaposed against each other in the opulence of the ship and the effort it takes to make it so.

I glance around the lounge, searching for Harry, wondering how he fared after the kiss we shared last night. Did it keep him awake far longer than it should have, or did he peacefully drift off to sleep with hardly a care in the world?

"Pardon me, miss."

I turn at the sound of the voice. An older man sits at the table next to me, his gaze intent on mine, a smile on his face.

"I hope you don't think this is terribly forward of me since we haven't been introduced, but I wanted to congratulate you on your impending nuptials," he says. "I saw you and Raymond Warner together in the dining room the other night, and when I asked who you were—you both certainly made such a striking couple—I was told that you're his fiancée."

In the six months that Raymond and I have been dating and engaged, our paths have never crossed with any of his friends or business associates. Like me, Raymond comes from a small family. He's an only child, his parents deceased, and distant relatives an ocean away in England. While I was always relieved that Raymond did not come with the baggage of a large family and social circle that I would be forced to impress and convince of my intentions, I can't help but admit that it is strange that a man of Raymond's wealth and influence has so few connections in his life.

"You know my fiancé from New York?" I ask.

"Our paths have crossed before, yes. Socially, mostly."

What sort of functions has Raymond been attending that he leaves his fiancée at home? Is his time spent at his club in the company of other men or has he been hiding me from the rest of the circles he normally travels in because he realizes that my background isn't what I've claimed it to be? Even on this cruise, where so many of the guests have grouped together and paired off, I've never seen him be anything but cursorily polite to our dining partners. Perhaps his socializing comes, as Harry mentioned, when he's playing cards.

And then I remember what Harry told me about the emerald earrings. It was hardly the first thing I thought of after the kiss we shared last night, but I make a note to check them with the loupe Harry put in the pocket of my robe when I return to my stateroom later.

"Have you ever done business together?" I ask the man, curious about Raymond's affairs, which admittedly he has never spoken to me about beyond the basic facts that he works in finance and invests money in other people's businesses. I once asked him how he had managed to withstand the impacts of the Depression that had affected so many, but he merely waved me off and told me that a "girl as beautiful as you shouldn't worry herself with something as serious as business."

"We haven't, no."

So much for that theory.

"I'm sorry," I say. "I didn't catch your name."

"It's Paul Christopher."

"It's lovely to meet you, Mr. Christopher. I'm Catherine Dohan."

He inclines his head in greeting. "Miss Dohan."

I hesitate. "I'm sorry for all the questions. I was just a bit surprised when you introduced yourself. Raymond and I haven't been engaged that long, you see, and I haven't had a chance to meet any of his friends yet. I didn't realize he had any friends on the ship. He must have been excited to see you again."

"We saw each other briefly while he was playing cards last night. Your fiancé seems like a fine man, but truthfully, I wouldn't go so far as to call us friends. Acquaintances, at best. Still, it is nice to see him doing so well, to see that he has found happiness again. What happened to him was such a tragedy. We were all very sad for him." He flushes. "I apologize. I shouldn't have mentioned it. The man was clearly so broken up when it happened—well, it's understandable that he wouldn't want to speak of such nasty business with you."

"Please, Mr. Christopher. I assure you, whatever news you have will hardly upset me. In fact, you would be doing me a kindness to help me understand Raymond better."

"Well, it's just—when his wife died, it was such a tragedy. He loved her so much that it was a pleasant surprise to see that he had found love again after such heartbreak."

Raymond's first wife, Ava's mother, is a subject he never speaks of. He didn't even mention he had a daughter until we had been seeing each other for a month. He simply told me that his wife died of a heart condition early in their marriage—her loss too painful for him to speak of—leaving him and Ava all alone.

If I were the sort of woman who yearned to be a mother, perhaps it would have been a more natural role for me to assume, to care for the little girl as my own. But motherhood has never been an ambition of mine, and despite my concern for Ava and the responsibility I feel to honor her mother's love and wishes for her, I have no idea how to relate to the toddler even in the few opportunities I've had.

Worry flashes across the man's face. "I'm sorry—perhaps I shouldn't have brought up such a painful subject with you on the cruise celebrating such a joyful occasion. My most sincere apologies."

He looks so bewildered that I almost feel a greater obligation to give comfort to *him*. He has a kind face, and whereas so many seem eager to trade gossip like valuable currency, I get the sense that this man truly did think he was doing the right thing by congratulating me on my marriage.

"Now I've put my foot in it. My wife is always telling me I need to be more circumspect when I speak."

I wave my hand in the air. "Please, Mr. Christopher. I'm not upset with you, and I assure you, I will not tell Raymond that we spoke of his past. I know what a sensitive subject it is. Think nothing of it."

He smiles, rising from his chair and leaning over to gently pat my hand. "He's lucky to have someone like you in his life now. I am sure the two of you will be very happy together and that Raymond will finally get the ending he truly deserves."

I squeeze his hand, a smile of my own on my lips. "I'm counting on it."

The first thing I do when I return to my stateroom is pull out the jewelry loupe Harry gave me, using it to study the emerald earrings like he suggested. Without the expertise to know exactly what I'm looking for, it's hard to tell if the emeralds are fake like Harry said, but the bubbles he mentioned are clearly visible under the loupe's exacting gaze.

Harry has made no effort to contact me since he took my engagement ring, and I can't help but wonder if after that kiss, he's waiting for me to come to him and demand it back, if that was his plan all along when he snatched it in the first place.

I still haven't worked up the nerve to do so, even though I must. There are only so many excuses I can give before surely Raymond will realize that the diamond is missing. You don't lose a jewel like that and not notice.

Once again, I spend the rest of the afternoon on deck, alternating between reading and catching up on lost sleep, sleep winning out considering the lulling effect of the warm sun shining down on me and the gentle breeze as we roll along at sea. I can already feel myself acclimating to the boat's rocking motion, the unsteadiness I felt on that first night dissipating with each day. I imagine by the time we hit dry land in Havana, it will feel strange to not be moving so.

This time, as the sunset approaches, I retreat to my cabin to get ready for dinner.

I take a greater amount of time preparing for this evening's fancy dress ball than I normally would. The festivities are to be held in the B deck ballroom and it has been billed as one of the highlights of the week.

A knock sounds outside my cabin just as I'm finished getting ready.

I open the door, surprised to find a uniformed crew member standing on the other side.

"A note for you, miss. No reply needed," he says, handing me a folded piece of paper before taking his leave.

I retreat to the privacy of my stateroom, closing the door behind me, the note clutched in my hand. I'd half convinced myself that yesterday's missive could be chalked up to a case of mistaken identity since there had been no other communication, but now I'm not so sure.

I unfold the paper.

*I'm not feeling well this evening and have decided
to retire to my stateroom. I'll see you tomorrow.*

Raymond

I toss the note in the wastebasket, relief filling me. At least now I'll have a reprieve from the awkward explanation of why I'm not wearing my engagement ring.

Dinner is a quiet affair, the odious Mrs. Gregory and her daughter at our table once more, Harry blessedly nowhere to be seen. I can't help but wonder if after that first night, he's avoiding the obvious marital designs Mrs. Gregory has on him for a potential son-in-law, or if after his daring actions stealing her bracelet, he's decided lying low is the best option. Despite her mother's obvious intentions, her daughter Melanie is as quiet as Mrs. Gregory is loud, although one can hardly blame the girl for her reticence. It's clear her mother brooks no one stealing the spotlight, dominating the conversation at the table and ensuring she has captured everyone's attention.

For her part, Mrs. Gregory appears to be in rare form this evening, her thwarted ambitions placing her in ill humor, her focus zeroing in on each of our table companions at various points throughout the dinner.

I thank the heavens that I'm right-handed, given my naked finger, and do everything I can to keep my left hand in my lap lest she comment on the absence of my engagement ring. She's the type who would fail to notice her own missing gems yet seize on such an imperfection in another.

Her jewelry this evening is as spectacular as the emeralds, and I wait to see if she mentions the loss of her bracelet. But if not for the fact that Harry had put it on my wrist two nights ago, I wouldn't even know it was gone. She makes no mention of its disappearance, and for a woman who loves a captive audience, I'm surprised she isn't regaling us with stories of how traumatic it has been for her. Perhaps Harry was right, and its absence has left her wholly unaffected. Maybe she thinks it simply fell off and is too embarrassed to admit it, or perhaps she has so many exquisite jewels she doesn't even remember wearing it.

I spend far longer than I'd care to admit pondering the bracelet's fate—and that of the man who stole it. I understand taking risks and the sort of desperation that drives you to do all manner of things, but life is precarious enough as a woman for me to seek out risks needlessly. Does Harry ever worry that one day his thefts will catch up with him, or does he believe himself to be invincible?

"Where is your fiancé this evening, dear?" Mrs. Gregory asks, turning her attention to me.

"He isn't feeling well."

"Seasick, is he? Such a shame. It can happen to the best of us. I've been fortunate that I never get sick. I have such a strong constitution."

I make a noncommittal sound, skewering my prime rib, hoping she'll grow bored if I give her little to go on and move on to antagonizing someone else. It occurs to me that Raymond never mentioned what illness had befallen him. Was it truly sickness or something else that kept him from dinner this evening?

"When is your wedding, dear?" Mrs. Gregory asks. "You must have set a date."

"We only just became engaged. We haven't made plans yet."

"Hmm. Well, don't give him too long, you know. Men can change their mind at a moment's notice."

"Women, too."

Her eyes widen slightly and then narrow again.

"Will you have a big wedding?" she asks, ignoring my earlier quip. "You must have family and friends you wish to invite. Who are your people?"

There it is—the digging I expected.

"It will likely be a small wedding. I believe our love and the vows we take are the most important things. Everything else is unnecessary," I reply, ignoring her last question.

It's utter rot, of course, as I deliver the line with a sickly sweet smile, and *she* knows it and *I* know it, but if Mrs. Gregory has come to dinner hoping to play chess, then I am more than happy to oblige her.

She leans forward, her voice unnaturally loud despite the conspiratorial manner she adopts. "Take my advice—if you hope to keep him, get him to the altar before he loses interest."

Her words are so ridiculously insulting, as though I am somehow fortunate to be the benefactor of Raymond's attentions, that I open my mouth to give her the crushing setdown she deserves when suddenly there is a commotion at the edge of the ballroom, a familiar laugh, and I turn my head in time to watch Harry enter the room, a dazzling woman on each arm.

Each time I see him out in public on the ship, it feels as though I am greeting a stranger. The version of Harry who stood in his cabin and told me about his father, who I embraced, is gone now, that fleeting moment of vulnerability replaced by the playboy persona he has adopted on the *Morro Castle*.

The urge to gather my skirts in hand and flee the room after that kiss—and my reaction to it—is strong, but instead I am frozen in my chair, unable to look away from the fine figure he cuts in his evening dress, remembering what it was like to have his arms around me, to feel his lips upon mine—

Who are those women with him?

Harry looks across the ballroom as though he is searching for something, or someone, and I suck in a deep breath, waiting, waiting—

Our gazes meet.

Mrs. Gregory says something else to me, but I scarcely hear her, my attention solely on Harry.

This is not good.

Surely, someone will notice.

I need my engagement ring back.

I consider rising from the table now and approaching him, demanding he return my ring, but there is something about going up to him when he has a woman on each arm that feels like I am ceding a victory, and besides, it's hardly like I can demand the ring back in front of the other women.

Better to make him come to me.

With a tremendous effort, I return my attention to my dinner companions, hoping Harry enjoys the view of my exposed skin and the gown's low-cut back.

Dinner passes quickly, and I scarcely remember what is said, Mrs. Gregory's attentions locked on other guests at the table once more, my mind already contemplating my impending confrontation with Harry. He may have come to dinner in the company of others, but I've no doubt by the end of the night he will approach me.

We migrate from dinner to dancing, the fancy dress ball in full swing.

The band plays to a largely costumed crowd. Everyone is in a good mood, even some of the crew dancing with guests and keeping them entertained.

I fetch myself a glass of champagne and find a spot on the fringes of the party private enough to carry on a conversation but conspicuous enough that Harry can't miss me should he come looking for me.

I'm not there more than a minute or two, when there's a familiar voice in my ear.

"Nice dress."

I don't give Harry the satisfaction of turning to look at him, but I'm not wholly unfazed, my hand jerking slightly at the sound of his voice, the realization that he is standing just behind me like he was that night on the deck. The champagne in my glass tips slightly, the golden liquid listing closely to the flute's rim.

"I need my engagement ring back," I say without preamble.

"Of course. It's in my stateroom. Care to come with me and get it?"

His voice is like silk wrapping around me.

"Absolutely not. You can bring it to me."

"That's a shame. I need to talk to you, though."

"There's no need to talk about it. The kiss was a mistake, obviously," I hiss. "One that can't be repeated. It was late, and—"

"It's not about the kiss," he interjects. "Although I figured you were going through some variation of this throughout the day. It's about Raymond."

"Raymond? What would you have to tell me about Raymond?"

"He's not who you think he is."

"What are you talking about?"

"Your fiancé. Something is not right about that guy."

"I can't do this right now. We're in public." I turn toward him, startled to find my face inches from his. "Someone might overhear us. I came to tell you that I need my ring back, but this—meeting like this—must stop."

"Then come talk to me somewhere private where we don't have to worry about people overhearing us."

"I'm not going to your stateroom again."

"This isn't about that. I'm worried for you."

Harry makes an impatient noise and takes my hand, tugging me out to the balcony, and even though it would be the easiest thing in the world for me to pull my hand out of his grasp and walk away, I follow him, praying that our exit hasn't drawn the notice of any of the other guests.

He releases me just as soon as we reach the open deck. A few crew members mill around in the distance, but this is as private as we're going to get without being alone together.

"Just because we kissed doesn't mean you have some claim on me. You may be jealous, but—"

"I'm not jealous. I'm warning you from one friend to another. There's something off about the story he's telling you. Did you check the earrings with the loupe?"

"I did. I didn't know what I was looking for, but I saw the bubbles you mentioned," I admit. "I'm hardly a jeweler, though. Maybe all emeralds look like that under a loupe."

"They don't. You could put Mrs. Gregory's bracelet under a loupe and you wouldn't see anything like that."

"Well, good for Mrs. Gregory."

"Good for my fence in Havana."

"I know exactly who Raymond is and I have chosen him for my reasons. Please stay out of this. I can handle Raymond."

"You think you can, but you're wrong. No amount of money is worth attaching yourself to a man who is dangerous. I talked to some of the crew. Asked about him a bit. No one likes him. He doesn't tip well."

"That's hardly evidence that he's some questionable figure."

"It makes him an asshole at the very least."

I can't argue with him there.

"But there's more to it than that—there are rumors that he owes people money. The kind of people that, trust me, you don't want to owe money to."

"The kind of people you do business with?"

"No, I can't say I've ever been stupid enough—or desperate enough—to indebt myself to the sort of people who take a hand, or a leg, or a family member if you can't pay up."

I shiver.

"How did you find out all of this?"

"Men talk at the card table. In the right—or wrong—circles, Raymond's business isn't as private as he'd like to think it is."

"Have your paths ever crossed in the past?"

"I can't remember. He wasn't particularly interesting to me until you showed up on his arm."

I take a step back. "There you go flirting again."

"Not flirting, merely stating the facts."

"Are you suggesting that I end my engagement because of some cruise ship gossip about my fiancé?"

"I'm saying that if I were you, I'd investigate Raymond's finances. Did you ever figure out who left you that note in your stateroom?"

"No, I haven't."

"And what about the man on the deck who attacked you?"

"What about him? Are you suggesting that Raymond was involved?"

"I don't know. But I'd take a closer look at him if I were you. A man in debt who just so happens to be engaged to an 'heiress'? I'd be concerned if I were pretending to be the heiress in question."

"You just described a good deal of men in New York society and then some. The commodification of women, which has been going on since the beginning of time."

His brow quirks. "'Commodification'?"

"I told you; I like to read."

I know exactly who Raymond is and what he's capable of,

but there's no plausible explanation that accounts for Raymond being behind the attack on the deck. If we were married, and he had access to my alleged fortune, then I could understand how I would be more valuable to him dead than alive. But we aren't married, and he has nothing to gain from my death. And still—if Harry is right and Raymond does owe money to dangerous people, then he's likely desperate, and desperate people are capable of all manner of things.

"I understand that you're worried, and I appreciate how much you've helped me so far, but you must trust me on this— I know what I'm doing."

Harry shakes his head, a look of disgust on his face. "Are you really going to go through with the wedding? With him?"

"It's complicated. You wouldn't understand."

"I understand complicated, but you're right, I don't understand why you would be with someone like him. You're smart. However mercenary you may pretend to be, you're not foolish, and only a fool would believe Raymond."

"Not a fool. He's very convincing."

"That would concern me. It suggests he has some experience conning people."

"He's hardly alone in that."

"No, he isn't, but I would ask myself if that's alarming. A man who is adept at deception is hardly trustworthy."

"Are you speaking from experience?"

"Just offering a little friendly advice. I wouldn't be alone with him if I were you."

"Don't be ridiculous. How can I avoid being alone with him? He's my fiancé." I take a deep breath. "I can take care of myself. I've been doing it for a long time now. The last thing I need—or want—is a man doing it for me."

CHAPTER TEN

ELENA

"Wake up. Wake up. The house is on fire."

She can hear the worry, the fear threaded in those words, but sleep calls to her, her eyelids heavy, the desire to sink back into the darkness nearly all-consuming.

"Elena, please. Wake up."

In the recesses of her mind, she recognizes the urgency, like that moment when you remember you have forgotten to do something, but you can't remember what, *and she knows that she must do exactly as the voice says, that everything relies upon it—*

Her eyes flutter open, and the first thing she sees is the fire in her bedroom, climbing up the heavy curtains that block the light from the window, the flames licking precariously close to her bed in a curl of red and orange.

For a moment, she thinks she must still be dreaming, some horrible nightmare that surely she will wake from hale and hearty, her bedroom set to rights once more, the blue velvet curtains restored to their normal state.

The smoke fills her lungs, a cough wracking her body.

There's the voice again, a pair of hands grabbing her shoulders roughly through the soft silk of her nightgown, shaking her.

"We must go. The house is on fire. Please, Elena, wake up. He's trying to kill you."

Elena struggles to make out the words, to focus on what she's hearing, but her mind feels wrong somehow, like she can't focus, her vision blurry, confusion gripping her.

Her head lolls to the side, and her gaze drifts to her nightstand, past the Tiffany lamp, to the object resting there.

A cup.

She had tea after dinner to calm her nerves. One of the maids brought it up for her. She tries to remember who it was, if it was a member of the staff she is comfortable with, the running of the big house a laborious endeavor, the turnover high, but her eyelids are heavy, sleep overtaking her once more.

"He gave you something to make you drowsy. It was in your tea." Fingers curl around Elena's shoulders, jerking her to and fro. "I can't carry you. Please. I know it's hard, but you must fight it. We only have a few moments. The fire—"

Her eyes open again, and she leans forward, her limbs moving as though they are made of lead weights.

There's a name whispering through her mind, being shouted at her, but each time she attempts to seize it, to grasp it, it filters through the sieve in her memory like fine granules of sand.

What did Raymond put in her tea?

She lurches forward in the bed, her nightgown trailing behind her, another cough shaking her body.

"Come on," the voice shouts, taking her hand, propelling her out of bed.

Elena's legs nearly give out beneath her, and with her free hand she tries to grip the mattress.

A painting crashes to the floor.

Fire races up toward the ceiling.

They're going to die.

And then it hits her, the thought that has been at the fringes of her mind since she awoke—

Where is her daughter?

Elena jolts from her bed, a thin line of sweat on her body.

She's not in the sumptuous bedroom of her nightmares, but in her serviceable cabin on the *Morro Castle*, the smell of smoke still lingering in the recesses of her memory, the feel of heat against her body imprinted on her soul.

At least the dream came in the morning this time rather than in the middle of the night, leaving her restless and unable to sleep. She's always hated the dream and the memory it represents, but at least on this morning it is somewhat welcome.

It helps remind her of what is at stake.

She rubs at her eyes, hardly surprised to find that her fingers come away wet with the tears she shed in her sleep.

There is no justice to be had for what Raymond has taken from her, but this is a start.

Today the ship disembarks in Havana, and as much as she is eager for this next step in her plan, she also can't wait to see Cuba again. Her recollections of Cuba are inextricably linked with her memories of her parents, of the happy times they spent together, when her life was much simpler. When they passed away, it felt as though she lost the most important part of herself, and she suddenly found herself very alone in the world.

The streets of Havana are filled with the sensation of her hand in her mother's, of going to her father's office and playing around with his papers, of getting sweets from the candy store on special occasions. As she got older, it was trying on dresses at El Encanto and fantasizing about the life she would finally have one day.

Sometimes she thinks that losing them might have been easier if she hadn't been an only child. If there were siblings to share in her grief, then perhaps she wouldn't have felt so untethered when they died.

That was one of the hardest parts of being so far away from home in New York City—she thought the distance would make their absence easier, that if she wasn't walking down the streets she'd traversed with them the pain would be more bearable, but what happened instead was that it made it all too easy to forget those ever present details, the little things she'd once committed to memory that have now been erased by time. She can no longer remember the scent of the cigars her father smoked on Sundays, or the feel of her mother's arms wrapped around her, or the sounds of their voices.

Maybe it was the absence of a family of her own that made her so desperate to find someone who would give her the family she yearned for. Perhaps it was that need that led her straight into Raymond's arms.

Today, instead of the casual navy blue dress that has served her well for most of the voyage, she opts for one of the two dresses she brought that harken back to her past life—a vivid emerald green gown that looks fit for an heiress. She brushes her dark hair until it gleams, pulling it into an elegant updo. Her jewelry is simple and glass, but it's better than nothing.

While her dress is a few years out of fashion, it is so finely made that she doubts anyone will notice overmuch. She paired it with a wide-brimmed hat that covers a great deal of her hair and enough of her face to hopefully keep her somewhat incognito. This is one of the most dangerous parts of her plan, the chance of discovery higher than any she has faced so far—

But if she pulls this off, well—it will certainly be worth the risk.

She glances at her reflection, a sense of déjà vu filling her at the image staring back at her.

She looks like her old self, like Elena Palacio once more.

It just might work.

Her heart pounds as she leaves her stateroom, heading down the corridor, her sights set on the open deck, the papers she stole from Raymond's stateroom clutched in her handbag.

She walks out to the railing, a wave of homesickness filling her as the ship enters Havana Harbor. It's barely light out, the sun rising over the city, and for a moment it's as though she's a little girl again, as if she's been transported back in time to the Havana of her youth, the Havana of her dreams and memories.

It's risky to be on deck, to chance being seen, recognized, and yet, the simple pleasure of a Havana sunrise is too much for her to resist, even if the postcard view of the city she enjoys now is hardly indicative of the realities her people face.

"Beautiful, isn't it?" a familiar voice asks.

She turns in time to see Julio walking toward her. She hasn't seen him since they danced on deck together, most of her time spent confined to her cabin to avoid the other guests. Maybe when this is all over, she can take a cruise and simply enjoy the pleasure of being out on the open sea without looking over her shoulder the entire voyage.

"'Beautiful' hardly seems sufficient," she replies.

She's traveled a bit in her life, but she's never seen a city as glorious as Havana.

"It's been a long time since you've been home?" he asks, leaning over the railing beside her.

"Too long."

"What are you planning on doing once we dock in Havana? Will you visit with friends and family?"

"I have business to attend to."

She wishes things were different and she could spend a leisurely day in Havana, exploring her hometown, seeing all that has changed in her absence. The memories she has feel as though they belong to another person after all the ways she's changed since she was last here. She knew little of the world back then, even though she imagined she did; she had no idea of the darkness that could lurk inside people, the depths to which they would stoop for their ends. She was a naïve girl when she left, and now she feels as though she is returning jaded and bitter.

She bats away a tear from her eye before it has a chance to fall from her cheek, praying he won't notice it.

Footsteps sound behind them.

They both turn their heads as a group of tourists walks close to where they stand, exclaiming over the sights before them.

Julio sighs. "It's a shame they won't see Cuba as it truly is when they get off the boat. That they get the beauty and not the struggle. Although there's beauty in the struggle, too, in loving something so much that you are willing to sacrifice everything for it. I must admit, it feels like a very Cuban sentiment considering how long we have fought to control our own destiny. How many people can say they love their country like that?"

"I don't think they want the struggle. They want the fantasy."

"That's probably true. What are your memories of Cuba?"

"My family, mostly. Before my parents died. My father was a doctor, and we did well compared to most, so we were fortunate there. Our homelife was happy. We were a close family considering it was just the three of us. I don't think I realized how much I would miss them until they were gone."

"What happened to them, if you don't mind me asking?"

"A car crash. I was at a birthday party, and they were coming to pick me up."

"How old were you?"

"Sixteen."

"I lost my parents around that age. It's a tough time to be on your own."

"It is. I'm sorry for your loss." She hesitates, realizing she's likely told him more about herself on this cruise than she's told anyone in a very long time. "What happened to your parents?"

"They were sick. Our whole village was. We lost many."

She doesn't say anything and neither does he, but they both stare out at Havana, and she can't help but wonder if it's different versions of Cuba that they see, all the complicated layers that make this country an elusive home where firm ground always seems just out of your grasp. She was happy here, at peace here, sheltered here, but for so many others like Julio, life in Cuba has been an unmistakable struggle.

"Why did you wait so long to return?" he asks. "It's clear that you missed it."

She hesitates. "I was married. When we were engaged, he

told me he'd bring me to Cuba, but after we married, well—a great deal changed. I learned that what men say and what they do can be two very different things."

She knows how tight her voice sounds; it's impossible to miss the rage, hurt, and disillusionment threading through just a few sentences. Strange how you can sum up years of unhappiness so succinctly, but there you have it. Her husband was a liar and a great deal worse.

With each day that passed in her marriage, her world shrank smaller and smaller until she was dependent on Raymond for everything, and the mansion they lived in felt more like a prison than a home.

It happened so slowly, at first, she didn't even notice it. In the beginning, he seemed kind and solicitous, and after having lost her parents at such a young age, it was nice to be taken care of a bit. Raymond was older and more experienced, but that was part of the initial allure. He gave her the stability she craved, until she eventually realized that what Raymond liked about their relationship was that she was young, and he thought he could control her, and when she understood *why* he wanted to control her, preserving her safety became everything as her dream marriage became her nightmare.

"You're not married now," Julio says, his gaze drifting to her bare ring finger, a question contained in his words.

"No, I'm not."

Elena glances up at the sky, wondering if her parents are looking down on her now.

I'm home, she wishes she could whisper to them. *It took a long time, but I'm finally home.*

She looks back at the city of her birth, and imagines that her ancestors are smiling upon her, that with their guidance and protection she'll be able to see her plan through.

When the crew gives the all clear to debark the ship in Havana, Elena's waiting by the gangway, eager to be one of the first guests off the ship.

No doubt Raymond will be quick now that he surely must have realized the papers are missing, so she must be faster.

She would give anything to know his thoughts; is he wondering about their absence, thinking it was a thief who took them or perhaps a member of the cleaning staff who misplaced them? Or does he now know the truth—or suspect it, at least—that she is indeed alive? Is he looking over his shoulder, waiting to see if she will come for him, or does he still not consider her to be a threat? Does he plan on disposing of her in a similar manner as the one he attempted, believe her to be weak and easily managed, or now that the papers are gone will he recognize her for the formidable adversary she has become?

She wishes she knew, but in the absence of certainty, better to assume the worst rather than risk underestimating him.

When she steps off the gangway and her feet touch Cuban

soil, tears fill her eyes, a mixture of joy and sadness running through her. When she left Havana after her parents died and headed to New York, she never imagined she would be gone so long.

She can't help but look over her shoulder when she reaches the dock, checking to make sure that Raymond's visage doesn't greet her walking down the gangway. There are a plethora of guests disembarking the ship, smiles on their faces and excitement in their mannerisms as they see Havana for the first time.

There's no sign of Raymond.

While the cruise ship staff discourage the guests going off on their own, preferring more organized tours that shape the guests' view of Cuba, there are thankfully taxi drivers waiting near the port to take passengers into Havana.

Elena hails the first cab she can find, giving the bank's address to the driver, the papers she stole from Raymond's stateroom tucked into her purse, the falsified identification documents she procured in New York returning her true identity to her—on paper, at least—resting beside them.

For one morning, she is Elena Palacio once again.

The driver picks up on her desire for silence, offering little in conversation once he realizes she is not a tourist and has no desire for a sightseeing tour. Instead, she spends the trip with her gaze cast out the window, trying to see if she recognizes the streets or neighborhoods from her memories.

Didn't she have lunch with her mother at that restaurant once? Her father used to buy cigars from that shop.

She went to school just a few blocks away from here.

She yearns to go by her parents' former home in Vedado, but the idea of seeing the house where they all lived so happily is a painful one. Without them there, it's hardly what she remembers, and likely the house has moved on and made new memories with a new family. Time hasn't stood still in her absence, all the changes in the city making her feel like a visitor.

That was part of her ease in deciding to leave Havana in the first place; she didn't have much family in the city save for her aunt on her mother's side, and Cuba was going through such a tumultuous time politically that it seemed wise to leave the country, not to mention the fact that her grief nearly overwhelmed her.

When she decided to attend university in the United States, she thought it would be a chance at a fresh start, an opportunity to make something of herself that her parents could be proud of.

But then, of course, she met Raymond at lunch one day during her first week in the city and everything changed.

The driver turns down another street, and they're in Vedado now, not too far from the home where she grew up. Just a few more blocks until they reach the bank.

She glances over her shoulder out the back of the taxi's window. There's another cab a few cars behind them, but it's too far away for her to make out the passenger or the direction it is coming from. It's entirely possible it isn't Raymond, that it's just another person going about their business in Havana, but the nerves are there regardless, the need to beat him to the money fueling her.

With her "officially" declared dead, Raymond will have no problem accessing the inheritance her father left her.

The bank is one her father used for as long as she can remember, the bank's former president an old family friend. Like her parents, he is long gone now, too, but her funds were transferred over to a new representative, one that, thankfully, she is unfamiliar with.

It will be easier to do this without someone she knows or who knows her family; possible only if news of her "untimely death" has not reached their ears yet. It's only been a year since the fire, and it took time for the investigation, for the necessary paperwork to come through even with the greasing of palms that likely took place.

While the sum that her parents left her is certainly a fortune to many, herself included, the bank has far wealthier and more important clients. Hopefully, her presence will barely register—at least, until Raymond appears and creates an inevitable scene.

She can't resist the urge to look over her shoulder once more, checking through the taxi window again to see if anyone is following them, if there's still another cab behind them heading down the same street.

It's still there.

Still too far back to tell if Raymond is the passenger.

Did he yell when he realized the papers were missing? Or

has he come up with another plan to tell the bank she is dead and take the remainder of her inheritance, the part that her father purposefully kept separate from the rest of her funds? Her father must have known that a young heiress would attract a fortune hunter or two. If her parents had been alive and met Raymond, would they have discouraged her from marrying him? Perhaps they would have seen the things that she didn't and realized early on that Raymond was far more interested in her money than he ever was in her.

And as much as the guilt fills her, the shame that she should have known better, should have *seen*, she's learned in the ensuing year since her husband tried to kill her that the blame lies solely with him. That the young girl she was, filled with grief and an irrepressible hope, was no match for a man of Raymond's skill and expertise.

There were hints that there were others like her—not long before the fire an associate from Raymond's time in England spoke of the tragic loss of a wife Elena had never known about. The man she had fallen in love with had told her that he was a confirmed bachelor until he set his sights on her.

She should have known as soon as he uttered that line with a straight and ardent face that it was complete nonsense designed to ensnare a vulnerable heart.

The taxi stops in front of a familiar building, and after Elena pays the driver for the first fare, asking him to wait at the curb so he can take her back to the ship, she steps out from the vehicle.

She feels exposed on the streets of Havana, as though anyone from her past life might come up at any moment and recognize her. It's silly, of course; surely, she's changed, and no one expects her here anymore, and yet, she can't help looking over her shoulder, convinced that eyes track her every move.

The cab that was behind them for most of the journey is still there, coming closer now, until it is two cars away, and then one—

She glances at the back seat, just able to make out the silhouette of a man wearing a business suit—

The cab continues, rolling past the bank and disappearing into the mire of traffic.

Her gaze sweeps the streets, searching for another taxi, but they're blessedly empty of cabs. Wherever Raymond is, she must have beaten him here at least.

Elena hurries into the bank, barely registering her surroundings, any nostalgia receding at the nerves filling her as she approaches the front desk. A dark-haired woman sits behind the desk.

"How can we help you today?" she asks Elena.

Her heart pounds, victory so close she can nearly taste it, her father's will, and the banking and identification documents in hand.

Elena's lips curve into a full smile.

"I would like to make a withdrawal from my account."

CHAPTER ELEVEN

CATHERINE

Feeling very much like a character in *The Thin Man*—or rather, wishing I had their skills—I wake early the morning we dock in Havana, nerves filling me as I don my least flamboyant outfit—a simple dove gray dress that truthfully might stand out more for its lack of ornamentation than blend in as I'd hoped. If only I had a fedora hat and a trench coat, but no matter.

All around me, the ship is rousing, footsteps echoing throughout the hallways and decks as everyone rushes to get their first glance of Havana now that we're in the harbor.

When I returned to my cabin last night, there was another note from Raymond saying that he was still indisposed, and that he would not be able to take me into the city. I scribbled back a reply of my own expressing my concern for him and my plans to stay on the ship in his absence.

Maybe he really is ill; perhaps there's something going around the ship. But if there isn't, if he is planning on venturing into the city without me, then I intend to be at his heels every step of the way. Despite what Harry might think, I know the risk I'm taking, and I won't make the mistake of underestimating Raymond—especially if he's as strapped for funds as Harry suggests.

Once I'm dressed, my hair tied back in a neat chignon, I leave my room and walk toward the gangway. If Raymond is lying about where he's headed, then he's eager to conclude his business and he's going to be off the ship early and quickly.

Better to beat him to it.

It's crowded today, many of the guests meeting for organized tours promoted by the ship's crew, others like me choosing to venture off on their own. From the conversation at dinner, it's clear many of the passengers have done this trip before, as they reminisced about the pleasures of previous cruises and the delights of Havana.

There are guides yelling out offers to show passengers the city, a steady line of cabs waiting to take you wherever you'd like to go.

I can't help but wonder if Harry is off the ship yet, Mrs. Gregory's bracelet and whatever jewels he's absconded with in tow to sell to his contact in Havana. There's a fleeting thought that my engagement ring might be part of his haul, but it disappears as quickly as it enters my mind. The jewelry is a game to him—a flirtation, of sorts—but I can't imagine he would sell it.

There have been no mentions aboard the ship of missing jewelry, no gossip among the guests that has reached my ears. Either he's very, very careful or he's only taken Mrs. Gregory's bracelet this voyage.

Another flurry of guests exits the *Morro Castle*, and I move behind one of the buildings, peering out from around the corner, scanning the crowd for—

Raymond races off the *Morro Castle* at a breakneck pace, hurrying down the gangway and rudely brushing past the other guests. He doesn't glance around, instead his focus is clearly on the line of cabs waiting at the curb.

I hesitate for a moment, watching him from my perch behind the building.

When I decided to follow him, I worried that he might notice me, considering I'm hardly a spy and my experience tailing people is nonexistent. Perhaps it was reading *The Thin Man* that gave me confidence—or ill-fated bravado, but either way, now that I'm doing it, I realize my worries were for naught. As distracted and impatient as Raymond clearly is, he wouldn't notice me behind him even if I was terrible at it. His mind is obviously on another matter entirely.

He moves with remarkable vigor and speed for a man who allegedly has been ill for over a day now.

Raymond passes me by without a look, and I take a deep

breath and move from my spot behind the building, walking slowly, careful to keep some space between us regardless of his inattention.

There's a loud boom somewhere off in the docks and he turns in the direction of the sound.

I freeze.

For a moment, I think he's noticed me out of the corner of his eye, but if he has, he doesn't react; instead he keeps walking, heading in the direction of the waiting cabs.

It's now or never.

I move away from the crowd of people, keeping my head ducked, following in Raymond's wake.

He hails a cab, and I memorize the plate, slipping into another taxi a few cars back.

It feels a bit ridiculous, the cliché obvious, like I am in a detective novel of sorts, but the words slip out of my mouth as naturally as I imagined they would—

"Follow that cab, please."

We wind our way through the city of Havana, but there's no chance to take in the sights or enjoy the view, my gaze trained on Raymond to make sure we don't lose him.

I'm certain Mario, the driver, thinks I'm a scorned wife or mistress following my lover, and I haven't bothered to correct his impression. He just keeps chuckling and shaking his head when I point to the taxi ahead of us and the circuitous route it takes through the city.

We hang a few cars back the whole time, wary of getting too close and sparking Raymond's suspicion. Mario might have thought I was ridiculous in the beginning, but I can tell he's getting into it now, yelling when a car cuts us off.

For a moment I think we lost him, but then I see the taxi turn onto a street up ahead.

Mario swings a quick right-hand turn, and then we're directly behind Raymond's car just in time to see him get out and dart into a building.

"Do you know what the building is?" I ask Mario.

"It's a bank."

I can't go in without my path crossing with Raymond's, and there's no plausible explanation I can give to explain my presence there.

"Can we just wait here at the curb for a bit longer?"

Mario turns and flashes me a smile. "At this point, I'd be disappointed if we didn't."

Five minutes turns into ten, and then twenty, thirty, while we sit outside the bank waiting for Raymond to exit.

I slink down in the back seat, careful to keep as much of my body as possible from being visible through the window. While we wait, Mario tells me about his family, asking me questions about my journey on the *Morro Castle*. There's an ease about Mario, a natural friendliness that I assume comes from talking to many people in his line of work, that has me confessing that Raymond is my fiancé, and when Mario's brow raises at the announcement, I imagine he is considering all sorts of salacious reasons why I would be chasing Raymond around Havana.

"Here he comes—" Mario interjects, and we both watch as Raymond exits the building.

Even from a distance, it's clear that he's angry, his mouth set in a tight line, his face red, and the expression in his eyes—

"You should not marry that man," Mario says decisively.

Raymond gets into the waiting cab empty-handed, and they speed off into traffic.

"Do you want to follow him?" Mario asks.

"No—let's wait here for a bit. He's probably headed back to the ship, and I don't want to run into him. We can leave in a few minutes to avoid him."

I sit outside the bank for nearly ten minutes with Mario before we drive back to the dock and the *Morro Castle*. He gives me his phone number and tells me if I am ever in Havana to call him, and then I step out of the cab alone.

I turn down a side street, the *Morro Castle* coming into view.

More than anything, I want to turn away from the great big ship, the sight of which now fills me with dread, and disappear back into the Havana streets. I thought I'd seen all of Raymond's faces, knew what I was getting into with him, but the expression he sported outside the bank . . .

That glimpse of rage inside him absolutely terrified me.

"Catherine."

I freeze at the sound of Raymond's voice, and then I see him, standing several yards away from me on the docks. I was so distracted looking over my shoulder that I missed him right in front of me.

"I thought you decided not to come ashore." I struggle to keep my voice neutral, to tamp down the fear building inside me. "That you weren't feeling well."

Raymond meets me halfway, closing the distance between us.

His lips are cold as ice as he presses a perfunctory kiss to my cheek.

"I changed my mind. I had some urgent business in Havana. You should have waited for me to return before venturing into the city on your own."

He looks calmer now than he did leaving the bank, but I get the sense that he's keeping a tight leash on his emotions and straining to do so.

"Are you angry with me?" I ask, Mario's earlier warning in my mind.

You should not marry that man.

Raymond smiles, the effect strangely chilling. There's no joy in the expression, no warmth; rather it appears unnatural on his face, his eyes hard.

"Of course not. I was worried, though. It isn't safe here in the city for you to go out alone. If something happened to you, I'd never forgive myself."

"I didn't think you'd mind if I ventured off the ship. I'm sorry. After hearing the other guests speak of their previous visits to Cuba, I was curious to see the country for myself. I never wished to worry you, though. Are you feeling better? How was your morning in Havana?"

"Disappointing. But then again, I shouldn't be surprised I didn't enjoy it considering you weren't with me."

At the beginning of our courtship, Raymond was romantic, often flattering me as he's doing now. But after we became engaged, those occasions lessened considerably, and his romantic ardor dimmed. To see it back in full force—

"Are you ready to return to the boat?" he asks, holding his arm out to me.

I nod, reluctant to touch him. It's Tuesday and we're due into New York Saturday morning. I just have to make it until then. That's what I keep telling myself, at least.

"Have you noticed anything missing from your cabin lately?" Raymond asks me as we walk back to the *Morro Castle*.

"W—what do you mean?" My right hand is on his arm, my left hand to my side, but if he's noticed my engagement ring is missing, I'll have to think of a quick explanation.

"Someone has been in my cabin."

"Why do you say that?"

He's silent for a moment, and I almost think he isn't going to respond when he replies, "Some papers are gone. Important documents."

"Related to your business interests?" I ask, struggling to keep my voice casual.

He gives me a curt nod.

"Did you report it to the crew?"

"No."

"Maybe they weren't stolen. Perhaps they were misplaced or accidentally thrown away."

He stops, his gaze sharpening as he stares at me. "Why would you say that?"

"It just seems like the *Morro Castle* is a safe ship. I wouldn't think they would have problems with theft."

He glances down at my left hand. "Where's your engagement ring?"

Damn.

"I put it in the safe in the purser's office," I lie, my heart pounding. "It's so beautiful and I was worried something would happen to it."

"That was probably wise. Speaking of our engagement— I'm going to talk to the captain. I think we should get married on the ship before we arrive in New York."

For a moment, I'm convinced I misheard him.

"What do you mean?"

When he proposed, we had a brief conversation about getting married in New York City, but there was absolutely no suggestion that we would get married on the *Morro Castle*.

"We can have the ceremony on the ship with a few guests

as witnesses, and then once we arrive in the city, we can plan a larger reception. What's the point in waiting anyway? Better to do it now."

"Are you sure—I just—" I wrack my brain for any plausible excuse I can come up with to get out of this. There is no way I can marry him onboard the *Morro Castle*. "I had always envisioned us marrying in a church," I plead. "After all, I'm only going to do this once. I want it to be perfect. I haven't even found a dress yet. Our wedding is going to be the happiest day of my life."

There. That sounds like the sort of thing a blushing bride would say. Surely, he can't argue with that logic.

"I love you, Catherine. I don't want to wait anymore. I want nothing more than for me to be able to call you my wife. I won't take no for an answer. I'll speak to the captain as soon as possible."

A chill slides down my spine.

What am I going to do now?

Mario's earlier words when we saw Raymond exit the bank come back to me once more.

You should not marry that man.

CHAPTER TWELVE

ELENA

She rides in a cab to her aunt's house in Havana, the satchel of money she received from the bank sitting beside her on the seat.

It was easier than she had expected to withdraw her funds, the identity documents Miguel procured for her in New York to replace the ones she lost after she fled the fire doing the trick. The whole time, she feared Raymond would appear and spoil the whole thing, but he never did.

Elena can only imagine the scene that must have ensued after he arrived at the bank and realized the money was gone.

She glances behind her several times throughout the cab ride, asking the driver to take a long, circuitous route to her aunt's house, hoping the precautions are enough to keep her whereabouts from Raymond.

Perhaps it's overkill—likely it is—but she gave him so many chances before, believed that the first few attempts on her life were accidents, that now she'd rather be cautious than risk it.

She doubts he remembers where her aunt lives in Havana, and had he realized Elena was alive sooner, he might have been able to hire a private detective to track Aunt Marta down. But now time is not on his side, and considering his days are numbered, she prays her aunt will be safe.

Marta is the only family she has left and one of the few people she trusts.

The taxi turns down the street, Marta's house coming into view. Elena hasn't been here since she left Havana for New York City when she was eighteen, but seeing it again transports her back to the two years when she lived with her aunt after her parents died.

Marta and Elena's mother were never particularly close— their personalities too different, the six-year age gap between them setting them on different courses in distinct phases of their lives, but she'll never forget the kindness her aunt showed her when she became an orphan, Marta's willingness to take in her older sister's daughter an extraordinary thing.

After the fire, Elena wrote Marta a letter so that she would know that she was alive. Without the funds Marta sent her, the contact with Miguel in New York, Elena never would have been able to survive in the city, would not have been able to afford the passage on the *Morro Castle*, the documents she needed to start over, or the funding for the other parts of her plan.

Elena pays the driver and exits the cab, the satchel filled with her inheritance clutched in her hand. There's something about coming back here again that feels like she's crossing a finish line of sorts, as though she survived the worst Raymond threw at her and is almost home free.

She approaches her aunt's front door, tears filling her eyes. She did the same walk nearly six years earlier, her suitcase in hand, when she moved in with Marta after her parents passed away. Marta never had children of her own, and Elena always got the impression that she didn't want them. While she wasn't as warm or affectionate as Elena's mother was, she was steady, and over the course of the last year Elena has loved and appreciated that about Marta more than anything. In her greatest moments of need, Marta has been there for her, unquestioning and unwavering.

She owes her everything.

Elena knocks on the door, waiting on the front step until it swings open, and there she is—her aunt—standing on the other side of the threshold.

For a moment, they stare at each other, neither one of them speaking as they process the years between them, all that has transpired since they last saw each other. It was Marta who encouraged Elena to go to university, to study teaching, to have a career for herself. Marta who drove her to the airport when she left for college in the United States. It was Marta who wrote her a letter when Elena told her that she had met Raymond and was getting married after just three months of courtship and begged Elena to reconsider, to finish her education first, to take more time before rushing into marriage with a man she barely knew and at such a young age.

If only she had listened.

Tears drift down her cheeks, and Elena steps forward, wrapping her arms around her aunt.

"I'm sorry. I'm so sorry for everything."

Marta hugs her back tightly. "Oh, Elena. There's nothing you should be sorry for," she whispers. "I'm just glad you're home."

She releases Elena, pulling back and studying her face. "Are you alright? Did you get what you came for?"

Elena nods, gesturing toward the heavy satchel in her hand.

She follows her aunt through the house after Marta shuts the front door, the rooms largely unchanged since they last saw each other. Cuba has been hit hard by the economic depression that has plagued the United States, and while her aunt has lived more comfortably than many, the furnishings are worn in places, hints of difficulties here, too.

Guilt floods her when she thinks of the money Marta has sent her, the assistance she has offered when she has likely been struggling herself. Hopefully, the money will help her, too.

They sit together in the living room on the very couch where Elena once opened her college admissions letter.

She hands the satchel to her aunt. "Can you keep this somewhere safe for me? I don't want to risk it being on the *Morro Castle*. By now, Raymond has surely realized I'm alive, and I worry he'll tear the ship apart looking for it. I've set aside a little for my needs in the next few weeks, but I'd feel better if you kept the rest of it safe.

"I can't thank you enough for what you've done for me so far. I was so afraid after the fire, and if you hadn't helped me, I would have been lost. I want you to take some of the money so I can pay you back for all you've done for me. My father left me more than I can possibly spend, and you've been more than generous with me."

"I'm not taking your money. Not when you need it."

"Please. It's important to me. It's what my parents would have wanted, too."

"Your parents wanted me to take care of you if something happened to them. I can't help but feel like I've failed them there."

"None of this was your fault. You did everything you could to advise me and to warn me. I was the one who didn't listen."

"How could you have known what kind of man you were marrying? I was so worried that you wouldn't finish your degree, that you would be reliant on a man for money, that he might be after the fortune your parents left you. The worst thing

I imagined was the idea that you might be in a loveless marriage where you weren't respected. I never envisioned it would turn out the way it has, that your husband would be such a monster.

"I'm afraid for you. Afraid of what he'll do to you. You barely escaped him with your life intact the last time. Don't give him another chance to kill you. Stay here with me instead. Please."

"You know I can't. Not yet."

There are things she allows herself to remember—her memories of home, her love for her parents—and there are things she cannot bear to think of, her grief swallowing her whole.

"He must pay the price for what he's done," Elena vows. "It wasn't just me. He was married before. She died, too. If he's done this to me and another woman, who's to say there aren't more? That he isn't capable of anything?"

"Why can't you go to the police, why can't—"

"I have no proof of anything. And I've seen how easy it is to discredit a woman. I tried once, you know. A few months before the fire. Raymond had me put in the hospital for two nights. He said I was overwrought, that I was imagining things, that I was hysterical. Honestly, part of me almost wondered if he was right, if my grief and loneliness had clouded my judgment. Why would it be any different this time? He'll say that it was all in my mind, that I was distraught after the death of my parents, that I'm not well, and they will believe him because he is a man, and he is clever, and wealthy, and powerful."

"Elena."

"I must see this through." She takes a deep breath, tears pricking her eyes, a wave of emotion filling her. "This won't end for me until Raymond is dead and my daughter is returned to me."

She leaves her aunt Marta's house in another cab with a promise to be careful and some pastelitos in her purse. This time she asks the driver to take the long way back to the *Morro Castle* so she can enjoy what might be her last view of the city.

Tears fill her eyes, and she offers a silent prayer that things will go well and she will be able to return home.

When she gets out of the cab at the docks, she glances around, half expecting to see Raymond waiting for her. She spent two hours with her aunt Marta, catching up on all that they had missed in the past few years, so hopefully if he was waiting, Raymond has given up and boarded the ship instead. Besides, if he is looking for a confrontation, this is hardly the place for it considering how crowded the docks are. If she knows her husband, he'll wait to strike at an opportunity when no one is around. He's always been a coward.

She feels unburdened now that the money is with her aunt, her nerves over carrying such wealth around on her own great indeed.

The gangway to board the *Morro Castle* is up ahead, and she walks toward it, a mixture of regret and relief filling her.

She passes one of the buildings in the dockyards and someone reaches out, taking hold of her arm. She opens her mouth to scream—

"It's Julio. Everything's alright."

Elena whirls around.

Julio stands in the shadow of the building. Three children are behind him.

"I'm sorry for startling you," he says. "I didn't mean to, I just wanted to get your attention without making a scene. I need your help."

She glances behind him to the three children. Are they his? They're young—two girls and a boy—the oldest no greater than nine or ten perhaps.

"What's wrong?"

"There's a man I need to get aboard the ship. He's a military officer and he's in Batista's crosshairs. This is our best hope to get him out of the country and to save his life. His wife and children are with him, but I can't get everyone on board at the same time without arousing suspicion. Can you take the children? We've already arranged for him and his wife to get onboard the *Morro Castle*."

"What would you need me to do?"

"You'll bring them back to the *Morro Castle*, say the children are in your care—we'll pick a stateroom that has children to claim is yours—and apologize profusely for the fact that you have left their papers on the ship. Once you get them onboard, I'll meet you and take them somewhere safe so they can reunite with their parents. There are a fair number of empty cabins on these voyages, and we often bring people back in them."

He doesn't say it, but they both know she owes him for the favor he did for her on the first day in the cargo hold—letting her inside that crate without a fuss—and the note he passed for her. Even if she didn't owe him, this is the sort of endeavor she can't resist, an opportunity to help these people escape a dangerous situation.

"Of course I'll help." Elena pauses. "These empty cabins—you have access to them?"

He nods.

"I have a favor to ask then, as well. I can't stay in my cabin anymore. It might not be safe. Could I use one of these empty rooms? Would it keep my presence on the ship anonymous even from the crew?"

"It would. I can get you in one of those cabins if you'd like."

"Thank you."

He hesitates. "Just what are you involved in? How bad is it?"

"I'm not in trouble with the government or anything. Or the police. It's a long story that I'd rather not get into."

"Do you need help?"

"Just the room for now."

"It's yours."

He motions the children behind him forward, crouching down until he is at their level.

You can tell a lot about a person by the way they treat the

most vulnerable, and there's a patience in his voice and mannerisms that says a great deal. Raymond was never much of an involved father, and after their daughter was born, she'd hoped that it was simply his unfamiliarity with babies that led to his lack of interest, that as Ava grew older and he became more comfortable around her things would change. After all, motherhood hardly came naturally to Elena, and she'd never missed her mother more than in those early weeks when she was still figuring everything out and wished she had someone she could talk to. But whereas she desperately tried to be a good mother despite the inevitable mistakes she made along the way, the times when she felt like she was failing, Raymond never took an interest in their daughter, viewing her as an inconvenience and little else.

"This is Elena," Julio says to the children. "She's a friend of mine, and she is going to help you get on the ship so you can meet up with your parents."

The children nod solemnly, nearly in unison, as though their parents have prepared them for this. They likely have experience with being called to withstand difficult situations far beyond their years. Many have had to leave Cuba due to the shifting political climate, and she can't help but think of all the children that have been forced into similar situations, some separated from their families, others orphaned by the ongoing political violence.

Elena follows Julio's lead, crouching down to the children's level as well.

"What are your names?" she asks them.

The tallest girl answers first. "Camila." She's clearly the leader of the group because she speaks for her siblings as well, telling Elena that their names are Geraldo and Alejandra.

"Elena is going to pretend to be your nanny, so whatever she says, you need to listen to her," Julio instructs. "It's very important."

"We understand," Camila answers, her expression that of someone far older.

Elena can't help but study the girl, trying to imagine what her own daughter will look like at that age, praying that she will be able to see Ava grow up, that she will somehow be able to recover all the time that she has lost, all the momentous occasions she has missed—

First steps. First words. Tears that were soothed by another.

Elena rises, tears stinging her eyes, pushing the painful thoughts back to the deep place inside her where she keeps them locked away.

It's hard to be focused on revenge when your grief threatens to consume you.

Julio reaches out, taking her hand, the touch anchoring her back to the present, to the task in front of her rather than the past she seeks to avenge.

She turns to meet his gaze.

"Are you alright?" he asks her.

She nods, pasting a smile on her face. More than anything, these children need her to be calm for them right now. If they can be brave enough to be separated from their parents and flee the only home they've ever known, then so can she.

Julio releases her and gives her the name and stateroom she is to tell the crew is hers when she says that she's accidentally left her identification documents onboard.

Elena holds out her hand, taking Alejandra and Geraldo's hands in hers, Camila walking beside them. Julio stands near the building, watching them move away.

She would have helped them no matter what, given their plight, but it also occurs to her that there's an added benefit to all of this—if Raymond bribed any of the crew to be on the lookout for her reboarding the ship, at least the fact that she's now in the company of three young children will help throw them off the scent. They'll be expecting a single woman, not a nanny with her charges in tow.

CHAPTER THIRTEEN

CATHERINE

This time, I am the one who pleads illness to avoid dinner, Raymond's announcement that the captain should marry us on the ship making me feel as though the walls are closing in on me. Was this his idea all along when he invited me on this cruise? Or did his plans change abruptly in Havana and force him to improvise?

There's a knock at my door.

Is it Raymond come to tell me that the captain has agreed to marry us? Now that he's decided he wants to get married on the ship, is he planning on trying to take our relationship to the next level? The thought makes me sick, but it's the memory of his expression when he left the bank in Havana, the moment when the mask truly slipped, that sends a tendril of fear licking down my spine.

He looked like a man capable of anything in that moment. What will he do if I refuse to marry him on the ship?

I walk to the door, heart pounding, and glance through the peephole.

It isn't Raymond on the other side as I feared, but Harry.

I open the door quickly and he strides into my stateroom like he belongs there.

"Is something wrong?" I ask, surprised by the late hour.

"Do you want to get out of here?"

"What do you mean?"

"Dinner was deader than usual, and I only went because I thought you would be there. Most everyone ventured into the city for the night. Why are we going to spend a stuffy evening on the ship when Havana awaits?"

"I would have thought this was a prime opportunity for you. All those wealthy guests off the ship, their staterooms ready and waiting for searching."

"Maybe I'd rather take you dancing instead."

"Dancing?"

"You can't come all the way to Havana and not experience it. We could go to my favorite club. It's not the sort of place that the tourists tend to frequent. I promise you'll enjoy it."

I have a feeling I will, too, which is part of the problem. And at the same time, ever since Raymond's little announcement this afternoon, I've been eager to get away from this ship, desperately needing a moment of freedom. I feel like I'm going to scream if I don't get out of here.

"If Raymond found out—how would I possibly explain that to him?"

"Let's make sure he doesn't find out. I'll meet you at the docks in half an hour."

"I can't."

I shouldn't, but I want to.

"Come on. Live dangerously. I know a guy. He drives a taxi and he's usually at the port around this time. He'll take us to the club and bring us back to the ship when we're done. You'll be safe. I promise."

I want to go so badly I can almost taste the mojitos on my tongue. I want to let my hair down and dance, want to forget who I am, the promise I've made, even if only for a moment.

I take a deep breath. "I'll meet you there."

The Ward Line docks in Havana Harbor are busy at night, guests shuffling to and from the *Morro Castle*, workers loading and unloading cargo. Given the whispers of smuggling Harry mentioned, I can't help but wonder just what is in those crates.

There are men at the docks, too, some offering to take women disembarking the ship for a tour of Havana, others offering to drive larger groups around.

I hurry along the dock, careful to keep my head ducked low lest anyone from the ship recognize me. I don't see any of our dinner companions or anyone else that's familiar to me and

I can hardly imagine Mrs. Gregory venturing off into Havana on her own. Still—I can't resist the urge to look over my shoulder—once, twice—in case Raymond changed his mind and decided to spend the evening in Cuba, but my fiancé is nowhere to be seen.

At the end of the dock, Harry leans against one of the buildings, his tall, lean frame draped in a dark suit.

He has a smile on his face and trouble in his eyes.

Tonight is likely a terrible idea, but it is exactly what I need and want.

When he left my cabin, I changed from my simple day dress into a daring red gown. It's another relic from my attempted theater career, a dress I wore on stage in a minor role as a gangster's girlfriend. The production was awful, but the costume is quite simply extraordinary.

The look in Harry's eyes says it all.

He lets out a low whistle.

"I wondered if you would show up," he says as I walk toward him. "I couldn't decide if you wouldn't be able to resist the opportunity to have some fun or if you would be too scared to do so."

Harry holds out a hand to me.

I hesitate for a moment, scanning the crowd once more, but the coast is clear. Besides, everyone else seems too busy enjoying themselves to be preoccupied with me and Harry.

I take his hand, sliding my palm against his, a thrill filling me as he links our fingers together.

"I need my ring back," I murmur, remembering once again that my finger is bare. "I almost worried you might have hocked it in Havana with the rest of your haul from the ship."

"I wouldn't have done that to you."

"I know. I realized that eventually."

"I'll give it back to you tonight. I promise."

There's a cab waiting for us, the engine idling.

Harry opens the door for me, greeting the driver in Spanish. I can't understand what they're saying, but by their tone it's clear that they're friendly, that there's a history between them.

Once I'm seated, Harry slides into the back seat next to me and we're off.

Suddenly, a loud series of booms off in the distance makes the car shake.

"What was that? Fireworks?" I ask.

"Doubtful. More likely explosions. My contact in the city told me that things have been violent in the last few days. The homes of some prominent members in the government have been targeted. The tensions in Havana deepen every time I'm here. You can't help but wonder if there's another revolution in the future."

It's only been a year since the last revolution, and while things are difficult all over the world, I can't imagine how hard it must be to live in these trying economic times and to also be dealing with the constant threat of political violence and upheaval. It feels like the reality of Cuba is a world away from the frivolity of life on the ship.

"Did you go on one of the tours today?" Harry asks me.

"No, honestly, I don't want to talk about what I did today. Was your day productive?"

"It was. Mrs. Gregory's bracelet is mine no more, and I received a hefty sum from the sale of it."

"Is that all you took this trip?"

He laughs. "Are you chastising me for not being a productive thief?"

I flush. "No, not at all. Just trying to understand."

"I wouldn't overthink it too much. I steal because I like it and I'm good at it. I steal from people who don't miss the things they have when they're gone because they possess so much it hardly matters to them."

"Do you envy them, then? For having so much?"

"No. I pity the ones who don't value what they have."

When I had so little, I never could have imagined such a sentiment, but now that I've seen how so many of the wealthy live, I can't say that I disagree with him.

We ride in silence for the rest of the drive, and I content myself with looking out the window, getting a different view of Havana now that I am seeing the city at night. It's clear that the longer we're on the road, the more we begin to leave the areas more frequently visited by tourists and journey into neighborhoods where it looks like the locals spend their time.

The driver pulls up in front of a lively bar, patrons spilling out of the entrance, drinks in hand. The strands of a band playing fill the air.

It's the opposite of the *Morro Castle*'s grand ballroom.

It's perfect.

We dance outside under the moonlight for hours in between drinking cold mojitos, the band playing with gusto, and I can't remember the last time I've had so much fun. Away from the scrutiny of those on the ship, the threat of Raymond's ire, some of the tension unspools within me and I feel like myself for the first time in a year.

I've never been much of a dancer—no doubt one of the many reasons I was less than ideally suited to the life on stage I'd hoped for, but some of the other women take pity on me, showing me the steps until Harry and I are dancing the night away.

"You're a really good dancer," I call out to him when we leave the makeshift dance floor and sit down at a nearby table.

He grins. "You're just now noticing this?"

"I haven't exactly been watching you on the dance floor on the ship. Maybe if I had been, I would have wanted to dance with you," I tease.

He laughs. "Just how many mojitos have you had?"

"Not enough that you're going to have to carry me back to

the boat, I promise. It just feels different out here. Lighter, I suppose. There's something about that ship, all the glitz and glamour. It can be suffocating. If you'd known me before . . ." My voice trails off, the sentence unfinishable. "This is exactly the kind of evening I would have chosen for myself."

"I'm glad."

"Do you come here often when you're in Havana?"

"I've only been here a couple times, but I thought you'd like it, and while we could have gone to one of the more famous places—Sloppy Joe's or the like—I figured you would appreciate this more."

"Thank you. It's perfect."

I take another sip of my mojito, the tartness of the lime and freshness of the mint exploding in my mouth. They've been serving mojitos onboard the ship, but these are amazing.

I lean forward and, without even thinking about it, press my lips to Harry's.

For a moment, he seems taken aback by my kiss, and then he moves, his mouth opening to mine, and the kiss explodes.

I knew, of course, when I agreed to come with him on this little adventure that we were headed down this path. Nothing in this evening has outwardly crossed the appearance of us being friends, and for all his earlier flirtation he has been respectful, his hands on my body never drifting to more romantic territory.

And still, there has been an undercurrent as there always is with us, the sensation that we are building up to something, an understanding between us, an inevitability to this moment.

He sighs against my mouth, and I take the opportunity to deepen the kiss, threading my fingers through his hair, pulling him toward me.

The sound of laughter and clapping behind us interrupts the moment, and I pull back, a flush on my cheeks, suddenly aware that we have garnered an audience.

I take a deep breath, my heart racing. Harry's gaze is locked on mine, his lips swollen from our kisses. I'd be more embarrassed, but he looks as dazed by the kiss as I feel.

We're both silent on the drive back, and unsettling as it is when Harry is flirtatious and playful, there is something equally unnerving in this quiet, serious side of him.

When we near the dock, the taxi driver pulls over to one of the side streets.

"You get out first, so no one sees us together," Harry says, not meeting my gaze. "I'll watch you walk to the gangway from here to make sure you get on the ship safely. Will you be alright by yourself?"

I nod. "I'm fine, I promise."

The mojitos have already worn off, the return to the ship like a bucket of ice water has been thrown over me. For a moment, a reckless, glorious moment, I think about asking the driver to take us to a hotel, caution be damned.

I should never have kissed him. We were having so much

fun together, and I wasn't thinking, I just *wanted*, and now it feels like I've ruined everything.

"I shouldn't have kissed you. I'm sorry."

"Don't. Don't apologize for that," he replies, his voice rough. "Please."

I hesitate. "Are you coming back on the ship tonight?"

"I will. I'm going to wait a few minutes after you board, so no one connects us together."

"Thank you for this evening. It was perfect. Truly."

"I won't forget it," he replies.

It takes a great deal to keep me from looking back as I step out of the taxi, walking toward the ship in the harbor. The atmosphere isn't much quieter than it was earlier in the evening, plenty of the guests laughing and chatting as they board the *Morro Castle*.

As soon as I cross the gangway, I turn, unable to resist.

Off in the distance, Harry sits in the taxi, and even though he's too far away for me to make out his face, I know without a doubt that he's staring at me.

The hallways are much quieter than the docks were, many of the guests already settled in for the evening and the ones making their way back from Havana likely continuing the party onboard the ship.

I pass Harry's stateroom as I walk to my own, and it takes

every ounce of willpower to keep from stopping in front of it, to not wait for him there.

When I reach my cabin, I reach into my purse to pull out the key.

I stop in my tracks.

The door to my stateroom is ajar.

CHAPTER FOURTEEN

I stand still, staring at the sliver of air between the door and the frame, my heart pounding. I locked the door after I left my stateroom earlier. I remember doing so. Perhaps a member of the cleaning staff came into my cabin and forgot to close it behind them, but it's unlikely considering they had already turned down my room before I left for Havana.

I place my palm on the door, pushing it open, my feet planted on the other side of the threshold.

The light from the hallway illuminates my stateroom a bit, but I had turned off all the lights when I left, and the room is still largely cloaked in darkness.

Harry's warnings about being careful return, the sensation of that man's hands on my neck sending a wave of nausea through me.

"Catherine."

I jump, a shriek building in my throat.

I turn just in time to spy Harry standing in front of his stateroom door, watching me.

"Is something wrong?"

"The door to my stateroom was open when I got here."

"Are you sure you closed it when you left?"

"I am. After what happened the other night—the man on deck—well, I've tried to be extra careful with my surroundings."

"Stay here. I'll go inside."

I grab his arm. "Don't," I hiss. "We don't know if someone is waiting in there, if they're armed."

"I'll be fine. I promise." He tosses me a very "Harry" grin for reassurance. "I've been in worse situations."

He flicks on a light near the doorway, fully illuminating the room. It looks largely as I left it on the surface, but there are little details out of place—my book open-faced on the nightstand whereas I normally leave it with the cover facing up, a drawer that isn't closed but cracked open, a pair of shoes that I'm nearly positive I kicked off near the bed, now next to the chair in my room.

And then I can't take it anymore, my worry for Harry overtaking my fear.

I burst into the room behind him, my gaze sweeping over the furniture, any potential hiding places where an intruder might lie in wait.

Harry walks out of the bathroom. "There's no one here. Why didn't you wait in the hall?"

"I was worried about you. Besides, it's my stateroom. If someone broke in here, I'm scared, yes, but I'm also angry."

"Do you think someone broke in?"

"I do. Some of my things aren't as I left them when I went out this evening. It's small, but we always lived in such tight spaces and my mother worked cleaning other people's houses, so she taught me to be neat and tidy. I tend to leave things in the same place because it makes it easier to find them and care for them."

"Is anything missing? Any of your jewelry?"

I walk toward the box where I keep my jewelry, rifling through the different pieces. I probably should be keeping them in the safe in the purser's office given recent events.

"It's all here. Save for my engagement ring, of course."

"It's in my stateroom. I'll bring it to you."

I walk around, unsettled by the idea that someone was in here, going through my stuff. But to what end? Was it Raymond, checking up to see if I was where I said I would be? Or was it someone who came to hurt or scare me? I can't think it was a thief who would willingly leave my jewelry behind.

"The lock is intact," Harry says from his position near the front door. "I don't think it has been picked. Whoever came in here likely got a key from the staff. I'm assuming yours hasn't gone missing?"

"No, I have it here. It's been on me the whole time."

"Then again, it isn't the first time someone has been in your room considering the note you found the other night. You still don't know who left that for you, do you?"

"No."

"I'm worried about you. You could get off the ship now, get a flight from Havana back to the States."

"I can't—I can't leave the *Morro Castle*. Not yet."

Am I in danger?

Or was someone looking for something important?

Raymond's earlier words on the dock come back to me. Does he think *I* broke into his stateroom? Did he break into mine checking to see if I had taken his missing papers?

"Are you going to tell the crew? You should get the lock changed, at least." Harry hesitates. "Honestly, though, if someone did get a key to your room then it's just as easy for them to bribe a crew member again and get another one."

"Maybe I can change rooms."

"You probably shouldn't stay here alone tonight, at least. I can sleep on the floor if you'd like or stand guard outside your cabin."

Despite the stress of the evening, I can't help but smile at the image that conjures.

"I think that would draw a bit more attention than either one of us would like."

"Touché."

I take a deep breath. "Can I sleep in your cabin tonight?"

I wait for a teasing retort, but his face is perfectly serious when he says, "Of course."

***

It's after midnight when we enter Harry's cabin, marking the beginning of our fifth official day on the *Morro Castle*. In three days, we will dock in New York City once more and this will all be over.

That's what I try to tell myself, at least, as the urge to do exactly what Harry suggested and flee the ship calls to me.

I wait by the door while Harry retrieves my engagement ring, trying to steady my racing heart. I'm more unsettled than I'd care to admit by the invasion into my stateroom, but even as the fear sweeps through me, it's met by another emotion—a blazing anger. If it is Raymond trying to scare me, Raymond trying to push me into a rushed marriage, then there's a perverse desire in me to keep him from succeeding at all costs.

If I'd ever had the luxury of fear, I might indulge in such emotion now, but fear has never been a part of my calculus, not when the stakes have always been so high, when I've had so little and dared for so much, when I've walked a high wire for so long.

I take the opportunity while Harry retrieves the ring to study his room once more. The last time I was here, I was too nervous to fully appreciate my surroundings, to indulge in my curiosity about who he is in his private space.

Now I walk around the room, cataloguing all the details I missed before.

The sheets are ruffled on the left of his bed like he favors that one side, a mountain of pillows stacked against each other. A pair of reading glasses is folded on his nightstand table.

I reach out and touch the frames, a little charmed by the idea of Harry in bed reading.

"I see you're looking your fill."

I whirl around at the sound of his voice, feeling more than a little embarrassed to be caught going through his room.

I flush. "Sorry. I was curious about how you live."

"I think I like the idea of you being curious about me. I don't mind at all, although I fear the reality is probably a little boring."

"I didn't know you wear glasses."

"Just when I read."

"Do you like to read?"

"Not the same way you do—I've seen you on the sundeck with your novel. I don't think I've ever seen someone so engrossed by a book. I like to read nonfiction sometimes, when the mood strikes me. I think I lack the imagination for novels, although I envy you the pleasure you clearly get from them. Why do you love reading so much?"

"My mother." I sit down on the edge of his bed, a smile on

my face. "She loved to read. She was born in Ireland, and she always told me we were descended from a great line of story-tellers and poets. She used to tell me all sorts of stories she'd make up in her head, used to read me whatever books she could find. She had an adventurous spirit, even if she didn't have an adventurous life, and I think books were a way for her to indulge in her desire to travel, to live beyond the confines of what was afforded to her.

"Once I started reading when I was a young girl, it was like a habit I couldn't break, and I found myself escaping into stories whenever I could. Books are a marvelous way to reinvent yourself."

Harry is quiet for a moment that stretches on for longer than I think we are both comfortable with, the silence in the room begging to be filled with some idle chatter or meaning-less words.

I'm embarrassed to have shared so much with him, such personal, intimate details about my life and past, and he—well, I can't tell exactly what he's thinking, his expression inscru-table.

"Here's your ring," he says.

His fist is clutched, and when he unfurls his fingers, the diamond glitters in the light.

I make no move to take it from him, and I'm preternaturally still as Harry slips the engagement ring back on my finger.

His hands tremble slightly as the diamond slides over my knuckle and into place.

I don't think I've ever hated the sight of anything so much in my life.

Harry is silent when he's finished, and we both stare down at the diamond on my finger.

"Is this one fake, too?" I ask him, my voice strained even to my own ears.

"I don't know. I never checked. You still have my loupe. You could look yourself."

Did the person who went through my room find that, too?

"This thing between us—this flirtation—we need to stop," Harry says, his gaze on the diamond rather than me.

Surprise fills me. He isn't wrong, but all along he has been the one teasing me, pushing the boundaries of our relationship.

"Why do you say that now?"

"Because neither one of us can afford it. You and I both know this character you're playing is nothing more than a fiction. You're not the heiress your fiancé seems to think you are. What will you do when he finds out you're penniless?"

"And you're not a wealthy bachelor content to spend his days in dissipation and his nights with women who incidentally just happen to have extraordinary jewelry collections," I counter evenly.

"Sometimes parts of that are true."

I can hear the warning in his voice, the distance he is attempting to interject between us. Was it the break-in to my stateroom that raised this caution in him? Or is it something else entirely? I wish I knew.

"And sometimes they aren't," I reply, my voice soft.

Harry walks over to the bar in his room, his back to me, and I watch silently as he pours a drink for himself before turning to face me, his expression inscrutable.

"What happens if Raymond finds out you aren't the heiress you're pretending to be?" Harry asks again.

"Raymond won't care," I say, knowing it for the lie it is.

"You're that good?"

His tone washes over me, the speculative gleam in his eyes sending a thrill down my spine. This is a terrible idea. And still, I can't resist—

"Don't you wish you knew?"

Harry tosses back the drink, draining it in a quick gulp. "Perhaps I do."

"What happened to not being able to afford me?" I ask, goading him. There's something unsettling about this version of Harry who seems to be on the defensive. It's easier when he's the one making the moves, when I can chalk my poor decisions up to his influence. Harder now when I'm the one leading us down this path.

"As you pointed out the other day, I have a terrible penchant for stealing things I can't afford."

"Why is that?"

"Depends on the thing, I suppose. Sometimes I need it, sometimes I want it, and sometimes it's so exquisite that I must have it, the cost or risk be damned."

"Which one am I?"

He sighs. "You're all three, of course."

It's the honesty that does it. This ship, these people, this person that I have become who I slip on over my skin like a costume I can't shake. None of it is real. And I'm beginning to think I overestimated the risk I was undertaking when I began this ruse in the first place.

I want more of what I felt when we were dancing at that bar in Havana. I want to be Katie again, not this stuffy Catherine business.

I want—

"I want you," Harry says at the same time the words flutter through my mind. "More than I can remember wanting anything in a long time."

I have been many things in my life, but I have never been a saint.

In for a penny, in for a pound.

"Kiss me," I demand.

For a moment, he looks caught off guard, his normally urbane composure ruffled, and then he grins, the old Harry returned to me for a moment, a gleam in his eye. "Only if you ask me nicely."

I send him a look of mock annoyance, but under the exasperation is a thread of relief to see that despite his concerns, he's still going to treat me as he always has, that in this we are equals. "Could you please just not talk for the next hour or so?"

"Only an hour? My, someone is an underachiever."

I close the distance between us, flinging my arms around

his neck and hauling his body toward mine. In my heels, we're nearly eye to eye, a fact that I enjoyed when we were dancing, and triumph fills me at the notion that we are so evenly matched.

"No talking," I reiterate, pressing my finger to his lips just as the bounder opens his mouth, pressing a soft kiss and then a little bite to the sensitive skin there.

A moan escapes my lips.

"I thought we were supposed to be silent," he teases, and I realize the only way to get him to shut up is simply to fuse our mouths together so there is no longer a point where my breath ends and his begins.

It turns out, he didn't lie—he is good with his hands, and his mouth, and all the other body parts at his disposal. In fact, I'm fairly certain now that there isn't much he isn't good at.

Afterward, we lie in bed together, my head on his chest, a sigh escaping my lips as he strokes my hair.

Neither one of us has spoken since he took me to bed—or since I asked him to, rather. As much fun as he can be when we're bantering with each other, when he's playful, I like this version of Harry for the ease it brings. In his arms, I feel as though I can let down my guard and relax a bit just as I did when we were dancing at the bar in Havana.

I turn my head instinctively, his lips meeting mine, the kiss filled with a sweetness that unspools something wound tightly inside me.

"Where'd you learn how to act like one of them?" Harry asks me when we pull away from each other.

I stiffen out of habit, some part of my brain screaming that danger is near, the unmasking I've feared for so long here before me. I move out of his arms, bracing myself on my elbow, studying his face, trying to read his motives. Blackmail is always a possibility, but truthfully, if that's his game, I've already given him plenty of ammunition by tumbling into bed with him.

"Honor among thieves," he says with a twinkle in his eyes as though he can read the indecision in mine.

"My mother was in service," I reply, leaning back on the bed, tugging the covers up, the soft fabric brushing against my skin. It's been so long now that I've forgotten what it was like before, when I folded sheets like this rather than draping them over my body. "She worked for a few families, but there was one when I grew older—a family with homes in New York and Newport. I was invisible in that house, but I grew up watching them. Turns out I have a talent for mimicry. I listened to the way they talked, how they dressed, how they walked, how they behaved when they thought no one was paying attention.

"When I got older, I knew I wanted no part of serving others. I saw how they treated the staff, what that life would be like for me. So, later, I tried to make it as an actress on the stage. Thought maybe if someone noticed me, I would become famous. Go to California. Be in pictures, perhaps."

It's more than a little embarrassing to remember how easy I thought it would be, that I was convinced that having a pretty face, a pleasing figure, and a bit of talent would be enough to make me a star. I underestimated what it would be like, how I would have to fight and claw my way at every turn, and no matter how badly I wanted it, no matter how hard I worked, it was never enough, I was never enough.

"It didn't work out," I say. "I was in a few plays, but that big break never came. Eventually, I ended up in service as well. Another house, another family."

Another life.

"And you?" I ask, eager to change the subject. "The stealing?"

"A product of my misspent youth that stuck, I suppose. You already know about my childhood. In the beginning, I stole because we needed things. My father's paltry money only went so far and my mother worked hard, but life is stacked against people like us, and no matter how much she worked to survive, there was never enough to live on. I gambled some, too, but that was never where my true talents were. I'd be lying if I didn't tell you that there was a point when I could have stopped it all and we would have been fine, but I'm good at what I do. And to tell you the truth, I don't lose an ounce of sleep taking things from people who have likely profited off the labors of others their whole lives."

"So, you're an altruistic thief now?"

"Hardly. Just an honest one."

"Did it bother you, knowing how your father lived?"

"That he was wealthy while we were poor? Do I steal from the rich because I'm somehow trying to right the wrong that was done to me when I was a child?"

I flush. "I didn't mean it like that; not necessarily. Although I could understand if you did."

"Maybe that was part of it in the beginning. Maybe that's still part of it now. I'll be honest; I try not to think about him too much, try not to dwell on my past. I'm glad he's dead, and I'm glad I am where I am in my life, and right now that's enough."

"And this is a permanent career plan for you?"

"Hell if I know. At some point, I suppose I'll have to stop. Age and all that. But for now? I'm good at it and I like it. Kind of like sex," he says with a grin.

"It can't be easy, though," I muse.

"The challenge is what keeps things interesting. Some of these people pat themselves on the back for all they have, not acknowledging how little they had to do to get it. It's the effort you put into things, the work, that makes them worth it."

"Don't most people keep their valuable jewels in the safe in the purser's office? I'd think that would make your plans a little more difficult."

"Do you keep your jewels in the safe of the purser's office?"

"No, of course not. It's far too much effort."

"See, my point exactly. While that might be the safest place for them, you'd be surprised how lazy most people can be about their money. After all, so many of these guests left the real jewels at home. This is their resort wear. Not as easily missed or valued, fewer sentimental pieces that have been passed down from generation to generation."

"Not everyone on the ship is wealthy. For some, the loss is great, indeed."

"You're right. But the things I've taken—well, they are likely inconsequential to the people I have taken them from."

"And no one suspects you?" I ask.

I'm simultaneously in awe of his brazenness and afraid that one day he'll end up behind bars.

"I haven't been caught yet."

"That's not quite the same thing, though, is it?"

He grins. "No, I suppose it isn't."

"Getting caught—doesn't it scare you?"

"Not even a little bit. I don't think I'd like prison, but that's why I do everything in my power to keep from ending up there. That's why I'm smart about what I steal, how I steal, who I steal from, and the trail I leave behind. But the risk? Well, the risk and the stakes just make it interesting."

"Is that why you're here with me?" I can't resist asking.

"I don't have a good reason why I'm here with you," he replies, and I can't find it in me to be insulted because I understand perfectly what he means, the utter futility of this.

We are a terrible idea.

"I don't want to talk anymore," I whisper, rolling over so that my body is on top of his. His lips find mine in the dark, and while I know that I will have to sneak back into my stateroom in the morning lest anyone realize we are together, for the moment, there is nowhere else I'd rather be.

CHAPTER FIFTEEN

ELENA

After she boarded the *Morro Castle* with the three children, she took them to the cabin Julio had indicated, where they were reunited with their grateful parents.

Then she went back to her old room, quickly packing up her things, fear flooding her over the possibility that Raymond might come looking for her and find her before she had a chance to clear out of the cabin.

Her new room is in the first-class section, the hallway and décor much nicer than what she had on her own in tourist class. Julio told her that when many of the cabins went unsold on cruises, the crew would often either sleep in them themselves or they would sometimes hire the rooms out to people stowing away on the *Morro Castle*.

That Julio was able to extend his existing arrangement with the crew to a room for her is a tremendous boon.

Now at least if Raymond begins asking around, trying to figure out if she's onboard, at most he might recognize "Elena Reyes" on the manifest as a likely alias, but when he goes to her cabin, he'll see it has been abandoned and there's no record of her reboarding the ship in Havana. Hopefully, he'll think she gave up and stayed in Havana once the money was hers, but more likely than not given the fortune at stake and his ego, he'll tear the ship apart to find out if she is on the *Morro Castle*.

Unless she confronts him first.

Elena rises early from her bed, far before most of the passengers are out and about. At this hour, it's mainly just the crew who are awake, attending to their posts and ensuring the ship is ready for the guests.

This morning, it seems like some of the crew is still recovering from their own festivities in Havana. No doubt today many guests will sleep in after a raucous night in the city.

She walks out onto the deck, glancing around quickly, careful to keep her head ducked to avoid being seen, the risk of recognition too great for her to ignore. And still, it's hard to resist this opportunity to see her home for what may be the last time. If all goes well, hopefully, she will return to Havana triumphant. But if it doesn't, if death awaits her, then at least she will always have this, a final Havana sunrise.

It doesn't disappoint.

The sky is a backdrop of blues and pinks set against a burnt gold that illuminates the city, casting it in an amber glow.

She's never seen anything so beautiful in all her life.

"Saying goodbye?"

Julio walks up beside her, joining her at the railing once more.

"Something like that. Hopefully, not for good."

"Thank you for your help yesterday. Getting people out of Cuba isn't easy these days, and I always worry more when there are children involved."

"Are they safe onboard?" Elena asks.

"They should be. Leaving the country is always the hardest part—sometimes if you encounter the wrong person, you can't bribe your way out of it. At least on the ship, money can grease the right palms."

"How long have you been doing this—smuggling people out?"

"Since before the revolution last year." He sighs. "It doesn't feel like enough, to be honest. I find myself thinking about all the people I haven't saved rather than the ones I have."

She reaches out, surprising herself, and takes his hand, squeezing gently, offering some comfort she didn't know she still had inside of her.

"You're doing a great deal."

His cheeks redden slightly, and she releases him as quickly as she touched him, sensing his embarrassment at her praise.

Behind them, a child cries.

It starts out low, a soft plea, and then grows into a set of wails, each one louder than the next.

She turns instantly—the noise, the memory, some instinct inside her taking over as she takes a step forward and then another, before freezing on the deck, the blood draining from her body.

It's been three hundred and twenty days since she last saw her daughter Ava. Three hundred and twenty nights that she was unable to rock her to sleep, three hundred and twenty mornings since she watched those little brown eyes open, searching for her, a tiny fist clutching her finger.

She would know the sight of her daughter, the sound of her cries anywhere.

She reaches out, ready to soothe Ava, her body already anticipating the sensation of the weight of her daughter in her arms, the familiar baby scent that has haunted her for so long.

The girl's nanny shushes her, leaning down and picking Ava up as Elena longs to do.

Since they last saw each other, she's grown so much. She wasn't quite walking when the fire happened, content instead to pull herself up by the bars of her crib and stare through the railings, calling for her mama.

Now, she walks on somewhat unsteady legs, looking more like a little girl than the baby Elena remembers.

She has her mother's eyes, and her mother's dark hair.

The desire to go to her daughter is all-consuming, the need to be the one holding her nearly causing her to rush forward to sweep the baby out of the nanny's arms.

And even as she contemplates it, even as she takes a step closer so that they are only a few feet away, she watches as her daughter's tears stop, as she buries her face in the curve of her nanny's neck like she used to do when Elena held her.

It's like a blow to the chest.

Even though she can remember every moment with her daughter, even though the love she has for her guides every single one of Elena's decisions, to Ava she is a stranger. This unknown woman Raymond has hired to watch their daughter is the one Ava is comfortable with now. That's what he stole from her—not just her life, but most importantly, he stole her heart—her daughter. There is no justice for that, because even in his death, in her freedom, she will never be able to get that year back, will never be able to recover those moments she's lost. There's no price she can put on her daughter's life.

She doesn't realize Ava and her nanny have moved on, that tears are now slipping down her cheeks, her legs nearly giving out until Julio's arms surround her.

He holds her while she cries, while the grief she tried so hard to hold at bay pours from her. He holds her until the *Morro Castle* begins to sail out of the Havana Harbor, the ship stirring as more and more guests awake, the deck no longer a safe place for her to be.

He holds her until she can no longer keep the pain inside her, and she says—

"My husband is on this ship."

CHAPTER SIXTEEN

CATHERINE

My fingers stroke the worn leather spines of the books, my heart quickening at the sight of so many adventures waiting for me. When I first came to work at the Warner residence, I was dazzled by the immense library, more than a little scandalized by the fact that for such a grand collection it received such little use.

It's my favorite part of the house to clean, lingering over the massive tomes, dusting them off, preserving them. My mother would have loved this library as much as I do, would have curled up beside me in the bed we shared, her arm wrapped around my body until I was pressed against her side as she read to me into the early hours of the morning.

I select a book of poems from the bookshelf, flipping through the pages and skimming the words contained there.

One of the best parts of my job is the kindness and friendship

Mrs. Warner—Elena, as she asked me to call her—has shown me. She was the one who invited me to borrow whatever books I wished from the library, and so this has become a nightly ritual—

When my work is done, I pick a novel from the Warners' collection before retreating to my room for the night where I'm inevitably whisked away on another unforgettable journey in the pages of the books I read.

I slip out of the library quietly, careful to avoid awakening any of the other staff. Mr. Warner is away on business, but it still wouldn't do for anyone else to see me enjoying such privileges. He runs a strict, formal household at odds with his wife's generous and open nature.

I'm nearly up the stairs to the bedrooms when a whiff of smoke hits me.

I clutch the book to my chest, annoyance filling me. Likely, someone left a candle burning unattended, careless of the fact that they could burn down the whole house.

I turn down one of the long hallways, walking toward the smoke.

The book slides to the floor.

Instead of the lit candle I expected to see, I'm greeted by something far more ominous.

Fire.

I wake as I often do from the dream, my heart pounding, a line of sweat trickling down my back. I look around the room, searching, trying to get my bearings, and it takes a moment to calm my racing heart, to remind myself that I am not in that horrible house in New York City, that I am safe, that I am in my cabin on the *Morro Castle*.

No—not my cabin.

It looks like my cabin somewhat, but the details are different, the clothing more masculine, and—

I roll over and Harry is lying on his side in bed next to me, naked and awake.

"Are you alright?" he asks me, worry in his eyes.

"I overslept," I reply, lurching up in bed. "I was going to wake up early so no one would see me here."

I flush thinking of *why* I overslept, how little sleep either one of us got throughout the night.

Harry's lips twitch slightly, as though he can read my mind. He moves closer to me, so our bodies are pressed together, his arm hooking around my waist and tracing lazy circles at my back.

"You know, today is just a sea day. You don't have to go back to your cabin. I could go get us some food for sustenance and we could spend all day in bed."

It sounds like heaven, honestly.

"What about . . ." My voice trails off because after the dream, after the night we've spent together, I'm reluctant to say his name.

"You could send him a note. Will he even notice? Every time I see him during the day, he's playing cards and you're nowhere to be found."

He isn't wrong.

"Still—I should go. I have things I need to take care of today."

I rise from the bed, searching for my clothes, gathering the pieces we discarded all over the floor last night.

"Are you sure?" Harry asks. "You had a bad dream. You kept tossing and turning in your sleep. I tried to wake you, but it was hard to pull you out of it. You seemed really upset."

I have the dream often, but it's my first time since boarding the *Morro Castle*. No doubt it was seeing Raymond like that in Havana that triggered it.

"You kept talking in your sleep," Harry adds.

I had no idea I talked in my sleep, although considering Harry is the first man whose bed I have spent the night in, it's not exactly like I've had someone to warn me about it before.

"I'm sorry. I hope I didn't wake you."

"It's fine, I was just worried about you."

"There's nothing to worry about. It was just a bad dream."

"It must have been. You kept yelling 'fire.'"

I leave Harry in bed and return to my stateroom, turning down his offer to accompany me. In the light of day with the crew and guests bustling around the ship, it feels a great deal less ominous than it did at night when the corridors were empty.

My cabin door is thankfully as we left it last night, and I lock it behind me once I'm in the safety of my room.

For a moment, I lean back against the door, my eyes shut, steadying my racing heart. It feels like a seismic shift occurred between me and Harry last night. I'd like to chalk it up to fun—a lot of fun—but I'd be lying to myself if I didn't admit that it was more than that. That the attraction I feel for him grows with each moment we spend together.

I pull my dress over my head, my body eager for a warm shower.

I stop in my tracks.

There's a dress lying on my freshly made bed that certainly wasn't there the night before.

It's white. Elegant. Bridal.

I approach it as cautiously as I would a coiled snake.

There's a note resting on top of the dress, black ink against an elegant ecru cardstock.

The captain will marry us tomorrow night. Wear this. Raymond.

I lift the card, reading the words over and over again, my fingers trembling.

It falls to the ground.

I grab a robe from my armoire, belting it tightly around my waist, my heart pounding.

I walk to the desk, pulling out a piece of stationery from the drawer and scribbling a missive of my own.

We need to talk. He wants us to marry on the ship. Meet me on B deck tonight at seven p.m. before dinner.

CHAPTER SEVENTEEN

After finding that wedding dress, I couldn't bear spending time alone in my room, cooped up with my thoughts and fears. I showered and dressed quickly before exiting the cabin and finding an attendant to take the note to Elena's stateroom.

We swore we wouldn't risk seeing each other onboard the ship, that it would be safer if we were apart, but desperate times call for desperate measures, and I fear that somewhere along the way we've underestimated Raymond, and if we aren't careful, we'll pay a deadly price for it.

Once I'm his wife, will he try to kill me for my "fortune," too?

I knew when we hatched this plan together that the journey on the *Morro Castle* would be the hardest. During my "courtship" with Raymond, Elena was always there, in the background, giving me advice, her presence and the obvious pain she felt being separated from her daughter spurring me on. And even when I would come home from the lavish dinners Raymond treated me to, knowing that I had sat across from a man who had no problem murdering women for his own gain, even when I would retreat to the bathroom, heaving the nauseatingly rich contents of our meals together, there was always a reprieve, there were moments when I could take the mask off and be myself, moments when I could lean on Elena as she so often did with me.

But on this ship, in the middle of the ocean, somewhere between Havana and New York, it feels like the walls are closing in on me, like there is no place I can go where Raymond will not find me, no escape from this deal I have entered into.

I can't marry him.

The last thing I want to do is let Elena down, and there's Ava to think of, too, but surely, when we meet this evening, we can come up with an alternate plan.

I hurry down the deck toward the first-class lounge, the early-morning hour meaning many of my fellow passengers are still abed. On a ship that never sleeps such as this one, it isn't odd to find solitude while the rest of the guests are recovering from the previous night's adventures, but there's something ominous about the sight of that wedding dress in my stateroom—the feeling that I am living on borrowed time—that has me yearning for the company of others.

Someone grabs my arm.

"What—"

My words are cut off by the sight of a man standing over me, his fingers gripping my elbow, digging into my skin.

He's a big man, a vertical scar slashed down his cheekbone like someone took a knife to it, his nose appearing as though it's been broken a time or two. His eyes are hard.

"You're Raymond Warner's fiancée," he states.

I open my mouth to deny it, but the words are caught in my throat.

His breath smells like coffee and something else I can't identify, his face uncomfortably close to mine, my stomach turning over at the smell.

Every single part of me screams, "Danger."

I've never seen this man before in my life, and yet, he's instantly recognizable to me. He's the sort who swaggers around the city's meaner neighborhoods, preying on those who are in such desperate straits that they are forced to do a deal with the devil to survive, the type who makes his fortune off the misfortunes of others.

How does he know Raymond?

"Your fiancé owes me money," the man growls as though I've voiced the question aloud. "He's late. He promised me he'd have it for me the day we docked in Havana. I still don't have my money. You tell him if he doesn't pay me before the ship arrives in New York City, I'll take what he owes me and he won't like how I do it."

His voice is like the blade of a knife slicing through the air, and I jerk away from him, his hold on me so tight that it leaves me shaking like a rag doll.

"I—I'll tell him."

Footsteps echo across the wooden deck.

The man releases me as quickly as he grabbed me, my elbow burning with pain from his uncompromising grip. He strides away from me, heading toward one of the doorways leading to an interior corridor.

"Catherine?"

I whirl around.

Harry approaches, a worried expression on his face.

"Are you alright?"

"I'm—I'm not sure. Do you know who that man was?" I ask Harry.

"I was just about to ask you the same thing."

"I think Raymond owes him money." My voice shakes. "He seems quite intent on collecting it."

"Did he threaten you?"

"I think he was threatening Raymond more than anything. Apparently, Raymond was supposed to pay him the day we docked in Havana. He never did."

Was that the reason for Raymond's mysterious illness? When he cancelled on me? Was he hiding out trying to avoid paying his debts until he could retrieve Elena's inheritance from the bank in Havana? This whole time we thought we were hunting Raymond; little did we know that someone else also had marked him as prey.

As terrifying as that man was, if he's Raymond's enemy, then perhaps he can be useful.

"That explains the fake jewelry, then," Harry replies, his voice grim. "And the gambling. Raymond is not who he's pretending to be."

No, he isn't, and since he lost out on the remainder of Elena's inheritance that he was likely planning on using to pay off his debts, he's even more desperate—and dangerous—than I realized.

I need to see Elena.

"Maybe that man is the one who broke into your stateroom earlier," Harry adds. "He could have been looking for something to recoup the money Raymond owes him."

"The irony is I think my engagement ring is the most valuable possession I own, and you had already stolen it, so no doubt that's why the man is so angry—there was nothing in my stateroom to compensate himself for his troubles."

"You need to stay away from Raymond. Don't be alone with him, Catherine. Find somewhere safe—and public—to spend the day. Let me do some digging into the man he owes money to and just how much he owes. I can get it done discreetly."

I nod, only half listening, because while I am more afraid

than perhaps I've ever been, I've only gotten this far in my life by seeing opportunity where others see obstacles.

Rather than spend my day reading on deck, I choose to spend it in the first-class lounge, engaging in more conversation with my fellow passengers than I have in the entirety of our voyage. I sit with my back to the wall, my gaze never drifting far from the entrance, waiting to see if Raymond will make an appearance, but he never does—likely he's skulking somewhere, avoiding the man he owes money to. Gentlemanly of him to have shown the same concern for his fiancée's well-being.

Later in the day, I stop by the cabin Ava shares with her nanny Emily, relieved to find that they're both doing well and intend to remain in the room for the rest of the evening.

My head is spinning by the time I return to my stateroom to change for my meeting with Elena and for dinner.

I dress quickly, the reassuring sound of guests returning to their staterooms to do the same thing providing an illusion of safety.

After I've dressed for dinner, I exit quickly, heading for B deck, where I proposed we should meet. Maybe it would have been safer to wait for the cover of darkness, but on a ship such as this one, where everyone parties until the late hours of the evening, it is difficult to find privacy. At least now, most of the guests are busy readying themselves for tonight's festivities. Besides, the *Morro Castle* looks more ominous at night now that I know how desperate Raymond is, not to mention the possibility that the man he owes money to might accost me again.

I slip into the shadows where I suggested to Elena that we meet, waiting for her to appear on deck.

Five minutes pass.

Then ten.

Twenty.

Thirty.

There's no sign of Elena.

We agreed that I should follow Raymond off the ship in Havana when she went to the bank, that I would serve as her lookout and backup should she need it, and from my vantage point everything went exactly as we planned. Raymond certainly didn't look like a man who had gotten his way, not to mention the fact that he clearly didn't pay the debt he owed, and if our plan had been thwarted, surely Elena would have contacted me?

So why isn't she here?

Tears threaten, but I beat them back. We swore that no matter what happened, we would both stay the course, that at the end of this journey we would reunite at the bar in New York City where Elena had secured the necessary documents she needed.

There's still Ava to consider, and if Raymond did do something to Elena, then there's an even greater need for justice to be served.

I'll continue as we planned, and if I need to improvise, then so be it.

CHAPTER EIGHTEEN

After waiting for Elena, I retreat to dinner, equal parts afraid of the version of Raymond who will greet me and filled with anger and concern for my friend. Tonight, there's another dance after dinner, and the rest of the guests seem to be enjoying the festivities when I arrive in the ballroom for our evening meal, scanning the crowd for Raymond. It seems like the closer we get to the end of the voyage, the more everyone feels as though they must wring out the last drops of excitement and enjoyment before they return to the realities and drudgeries of daily life.

For me, the end of the cruise feels like a culmination, as though the tension that has been building these past six days is a powder keg ready to explode.

I find him standing near the edge of the ballroom, talking to a member of the staff.

Harry is nowhere to be found.

"Catherine." Raymond greets me with a perfunctory kiss on the cheek, and my skin crawls at the feel of his body against mine.

The crew member excuses himself, and we are left alone once more.

"The captain is indisposed," Raymond announces. "The crew assures me, though, that he will soon be better so that we can be married tomorrow night, the final night of the cruise, as planned."

He says it with the confidence of a man who believes he can control things like the health of others merely by the force of his will, as though the world won't dare to inconvenience him.

I can't imagine what it must be like to go through life in such a manner.

"It's a shame that he is unwell," I murmur, careful to keep my gaze cast to the ground and my voice low lest my emotions show. "Maybe this is a sign that we should wait until we're in New York, for the timing to be right, for us to have the wedding I've always dreamed of."

Raymond reaches out, grabbing my arm in an awkward embrace so that our bodies are close together, and I have no choice but to crane my head to look up at him.

"And I told you I don't want to wait. There's no reason we should. Unless there's something you're not telling me?"

There's an undercurrent in his voice that sends off an alarm in my head, and just like that moment when I saw him leaving the bank, the mask slips again, and I glimpse the real side of Raymond once more.

Something dark flashes in his eyes, and then it hits me—

Last night when I returned to my cabin with Harry and the door was ajar, there was no wedding dress in the room. But when I returned the next morning, it was there. Does Raymond know that I didn't spend the night in my cabin? Or does he merely suspect it? Surely, a man like Raymond wouldn't deliver the dress himself, but rather have a member of the boat crew do it. Would they have reported on my whereabouts?

"No, of course not. I just want our wedding to be perfect. After all, I've been dreaming about this moment since I was a little girl."

"And it will be. Did you like the present I left in your cabin? Since you were concerned about having a proper wedding dress, I had the crew take care of it."

"It's lovely, of course. You're too kind to have arranged such a lavish gesture."

"See? There's nothing to worry about. You leave everything to me and it will all work out."

Even though I shouldn't be, I'm surprised at how swiftly he's maneuvering me into this wedding, refusing to take "no" for an answer. Was this what it was like for Elena—did he try to sweep her off her feet, bending her to his will so quickly she barely even realized it was happening? Raymond can be charming when he wants to be—I saw enough of that at the beginning of our courtship, and it's only now that he's clearly under pressure that the cracks are beginning to show.

"What did you do all day?" I ask, careful to keep my voice from sounding *too* curious.

"I had to take care of some business," he replies, steering me over to our dinner table, his hand firmly on the small of my back.

Raymond isn't a physically large man, and still, there's something imposing about his manner, a ruthlessness that lingers below the surface, sucking the air out of the room.

And suddenly, I feel as though the ballroom walls are closing in on me, panic filling my chest, and all I want is to escape all of this.

I want Harry.

I eat largely in silence while Raymond answers questions about our impending wedding ceremony, inviting the other diners at the table to be our "guests" for the captain's ceremony. I smile like I should, blush appropriately, force myself to play the role of loving fiancée. I give the performance of a lifetime, but with each course, each hour that passes, I feel as though something is splintering inside me.

"I'm sorry, but I'm tired. I'm going to go back to my cabin and try to get some rest," I lie once the dinner service has ended, demurring when Raymond offers to escort me back. "After all, tomorrow is a big day."

I can't bear the thought of being alone with him right now, even in the ship's corridors.

"I'll see you at breakfast, then."

I laugh softly, for once grateful for this impending wedding and the reprieve it now provides. "We couldn't possibly. It's bad luck for the bride and the groom to see each other before the wedding, and I don't want to do anything to jeopardize our future together. After all, we're already rushing so much. I'd like to honor what traditions we can."

Take that absolute load of rubbish.

For a moment, I think he's going to argue the point, but like all gamblers I suppose he's been forced to learn the art of quitting when he's ahead, and he lets me go.

I exit the dining room, glancing over my shoulder every so often to make sure no one is following me, and head toward the tourist-class cabins where Elena booked her passage.

I knock on her stateroom door, praying that she is in there and that there's a reasonable explanation for her not making our meeting this evening.

Praying Raymond hasn't gotten to her first.

No one answers the door.

Heart pounding, I glance around.

Thankfully, Elena's hallway is empty of guests, and I reach up into my elegant coiffure, pulling out one of the jeweled pins tucked away in my updo.

The lock turns as easily as Harry's did, the motion coming back to me more freely now that I've had a bit of practice.

I push open the door to her stateroom, fumbling to turn on the light.

It's completely empty.

CHAPTER NINETEEN

I take the long way to Harry's cabin, careful to keep looking over my shoulder once more, to make sure no one is following me.

Is my reluctance to move our wedding forward making Raymond suspicious or is he so determined to have his way that my actions have little impact at all? I wish I knew.

When I reach Harry's cabin and knock on the door, tears threatening, I'm greeted by silence.

I try again, my gaze darting around the hallway to make sure no one sees me.

Harry answers the door.

Neither one of us speaks as he steps aside, and I cross the threshold into his cabin.

He closes the door. "How was dinner?"

"Interminable." I take a deep breath, and then the truth rushes out. "Raymond wants the captain to marry us on the ship tomorrow night."

For a moment, Harry doesn't answer me.

"Is that what you want?" he finally asks.

"No, it isn't."

Harry walks over to the bar cart in his room and pours us both drinks, handing me a glass.

I drain it in one quick gulp, the liquid burning a trail of fire down my throat.

I hand the empty glass to him. "More."

He refills my drink again, handing it to me silently.

I take a swig of the liquor, wiping the excess from my lips with the knuckles of my fist.

I don't bat an eye when Harry takes my hand, lifting my fingers to his mouth, sucking the liquid from my skin.

A tremor slides through my body.

A thread of desperation fuels me, a hint of temper and recklessness I rarely dare to indulge. I learned at a young age that I was born into a world that would not allow me to do as I pleased, that if I wanted to survive, to thrive, I had to play by other rules, to bury the parts of myself that didn't serve me.

I had to be careful, and calculating, and wear a mask when I went out in the world.

I pull my hand out of Harry's and take another swig of the liquor, grateful for the slow burn and its ability to distract me from his fingers now stroking my bare arm.

I cock my head to the side, studying him. "Did you know I used to be a redhead?" I point to my brown hair, my voice dropping to a mock whisper. "I dye it."

His lips twitch. "Is that so?"

I nod.

"Brown hair suits you. I imagine the red would, too."

"I loved it," I reply wistfully. "I had my mother's hair. Every night before bed, she used to brush my long hair. I loved sitting there while she would braid it afterward, loved looking at our reflections and knowing that I was a miniature of her."

"You loved her a great deal."

"I did. It was just us for so long—there's a bond that develops. We weren't only mother and daughter; it's like we were two halves of a whole."

"How old were you when she passed?"

"Seventeen."

"I'm sorry. That must have been hard."

"It was. Suddenly, I was very alone in the world. It was a terrifying thing to be a young girl in a city like New York. I tried my hand at a few things—acting, for one—before I found a job as a maid at a grand house. Luckily, my employer's wife looked out for me. She wasn't much older than me, to be honest. Maybe that's why she took such a liking to me. I think she felt very alone in that great big house, and she needed a friend more than anything. She took me into her confidence. We were close. I was her personal maid, but it often felt like we were more like sisters than anything else. I learned a great deal about society from her. Learned how to reinvent myself."

"What does she think of all of this? What does she think about you and Raymond?"

I turn away from him, staring out the balcony door in his cabin at the sea, the liquor glass dangling between my fingers.

"You're awfully disapproving, you know, for a thief."

"What's that supposed to mean?"

"I just figured you would be less judgmental considering your work, more open to bending the lines, so to speak."

"Is that what you're doing with Raymond—'bending the lines'? Because it looks to me like you've put yourself in a dangerous situation, and I wonder if the money is worth it to you."

"It's not just about the money. Things are complicated. What exists between me and Raymond—it's not what you think."

"Then what is it? Why can't you trust me?"

"I do trust you. More than most. But you must trust me that there are some secrets that aren't mine to tell."

"And yet, you're the one putting yourself in danger, taking on all of these risks."

"I promise you. I'm going to be smart about this. I know you're worried that I'm being reckless, but I know what I'm doing."

"He doesn't have any money," Harry blurts out. "I spent the day asking around—discreetly, of course—because I didn't understand why a man who allegedly had so much money would be buying his fiancée fake jewels, and when you told me he owed someone money—well, I saw how poor of a gambler he is for myself on this journey. There are some well-connected people on this ship and a lot of them like to talk over a hand of cards. That's where I went instead of dinner this evening. I knew he would be with you, and I wanted to see if I could find out some information when he wasn't around. He owes people money. A lot of money."

"How does he owe so much?"

I saw the house they lived in, know Elena's fortune was great. We always assumed he was marrying heiresses for their wealth, but never did we imagine it would be because he was in such dire straits.

"The Depression has hit so many people hard. It's a tough time to be in finance. Lots of investments have suffered. Besides that, he lost thousands the few nights I've seen him play cards. It sounds like he has a gambling problem and he owes the kind of money that makes you do desperate things. Like marry an heiress. Or worse.

"Did you know he was married before?" Harry asks me.

I hesitate. "Yes."

"His wife was Cuban. Wealthy. An only child—an orphan in fact—of a doctor from a prestigious family in Havana. Do you know how she died?"

"There was a fire," I say, realizing how very faint my voice sounds to my own ears, the horror of that night rushing toward me.

"What if the reason he wants to marry you now is because he thinks you're an heiress?

That's exactly why he wants to marry me.

"What do you think he'll do when he finds out you're not?"

Kill me.

Harry takes a deep breath. "I need to tell you something. I know you think I'm jealous, and truthfully, yes—I am—but this isn't about that. While you were at dinner, I broke into the ship's safe."

"You did what?"

He walks over to his stateroom desk and picks up a stack of papers, holding them out to me wordlessly.

"You need to read this."

It takes a minute for the words in front of me to register, for me to realize what I'm looking at, for the last puzzle piece to slide into place.

It's a life insurance policy.

For my life.

And Raymond's the beneficiary.

CHAPTER TWENTY

ELENA

"Where's Ava? I must find my daughter."

Katie wraps her arms around Elena, pulling her through the bedroom doorway, and together they head for the stairs, the smoke spilling out behind them.

"She's not in the house," Katie replies.

That's right. Elena remembers now. She's in the country. Raymond insisted that she stay there, that Elena's nerves were too fragile, that she needed a break from the baby, that she needed some time to rest and get well. He'd hired another nanny, the fourth one this year. They had argued about that, too, but Raymond had left her with no choice. He liked hiring and firing the nannies when Elena became close to them, when she found someone she trusted to take care of her daughter. It's part of why she's been so careful to keep her friendship with Katie a secret.

Coughs wrack their bodies as they head down the stairs.

She can hear the staff milling around through the chaos, the smoke so thick that she can barely see around her, her eyes burning.

The front door is just a few steps ahead of them, and Elena struggles to keep walking, exhaustion filling her, the desire to collapse on the floor overtaking her.

What's next? What else will Raymond do to her? And Ava—is her little girl safe? He wouldn't hurt his daughter, would he?

"Come on. Just a little bit farther," Katie calls out, and then they're outside finally, fresh air filling her lungs.

Onlookers crowd in front of the mansion, the fire spread to the roof now.

The wail of a siren comes down the street, a fire truck racing toward them.

Katie pulls Elena out of the way, and they sit on the curb, huddled together. It's cold outside, a chill in the October air, Elena's limbs feeling as though they're waking up with each minute that passes by.

One of the firemen walks over to them. "Were you in the house? What happened?" he asks. "Is there anyone still in there?"

Elena opens her mouth to answer him, dread filling her. Last time she tried to tell someone about her suspicions and fears that Raymond was trying to hurt her, he convinced the police that she was paranoid and had her sent to a sanitarium for a few days. He's been hinting more and more that she could be a danger to her daughter, that she should be more careful, that she's prone to bouts of hysteria.

She wants to tell the man the truth, that she now knows without a doubt that her husband is trying to kill her, but she's afraid he won't believe her, like the others, and that the next time Raymond tries to kill her, he'll succeed.

Katie stands up suddenly.

"I was in the house," she answers. "I'm a maid." She hesitates, and then her voice shakes, tears filling her eyes. "The mistress of the house—it started in her bedroom. I tried to get her out, but—I couldn't—the fire—she died."

Tears spill down Katie's cheeks and she sinks back down to the curb, wrapping her arms around her body.

"And you?" he asks Elena. "Were you in the house?"

Katie reaches out, squeezing Elena's hand, and suddenly Elena sees it, a way out for herself, a freedom she'd only ever dreamed of and perhaps the best hope she has for her and Ava to come out of this safely.

Elena shakes her head. "No—I work at the neighbor's house over there. I saw the fire and I went in and tried to help."

He asks Katie a few more questions, and then he leaves them alone.

"We need to get out of here," Katie whispers. "Need to get you somewhere safe."

Elena looks down at her bare feet on the cold New York sidewalk, her body wrapped in a blanket over the nightdress she was wearing when she fell asleep. Maybe if the fireman had looked closer, he would have realized that she was dressed too finely to be a maid in the neighboring house, would have noticed the diamond wedding band still on her finger.

She's walking away from her life with almost nothing, but at least the ring will go a long way to helping once she sells it.

And then anger fills her, sharp and bright, breaking through the drugs he slipped in her tea, the shock of the fire, everything, and in that moment, she thinks she will do whatever it takes to see Raymond pay for what he has done to her, the fortune he has stolen from her, the dreams he has ruined.

She will do anything to get her daughter back.

Her grief is a roar building inside her chest, desperate to break free.

CHAPTER TWENTY-ONE

CATHERINE

If we hoped for good weather on our final day at sea, we are clearly to be disappointed. It's rainy and miserable outside, driving everyone indoors to pursue other activities. I wake in Harry's room once more, leaving him in the early hours to return to my own stateroom and begin packing my suitcases in preparation for us docking in New York tomorrow.

The white wedding dress hangs in my closet taunting me. Everything hinges on tonight.

I thought that if we stayed a few steps ahead of Raymond and he never saw us coming, we'd be safe, but that seems impossible now that he's changed the game and moved up the wedding date, not to mention the life insurance policy.

We always assured ourselves that I would be safe on the ship with him if we weren't married, as long as he didn't have access to my alleged fortune, but we never considered that he would take a life insurance policy out on me, that I would be valuable to him dead whether we were married or not.

I've no doubt that Raymond was the one behind the attack that first night on the ship. And now that the man he owes money to is getting so impatient that he's threatening me, what will Raymond do to appease him?

When I'm finished packing, I leave my cabin in search of Harry.

"It's unlocked. Come in," he calls out after I knock on his stateroom, the sound muffled by the heavy wooden door between us.

I'm greeted by the sight of Harry lying in bed, his chest bare, the sheets pooled around his waist.

I close the door behind me quickly.

"Do you always answer your stateroom door like that?" I ask. "What if it wasn't me?"

"Then someone would have gotten a good view."

I roll my eyes.

He grins, even if the amusement doesn't quite reach his gaze. "Relax. I knew it was you. I recognized your knock."

"How can you recognize my knock?"

"The number of raps you do. The tempo. The fact that I can basically feel your indecision and tension through the door."

"I have a lot on my mind," I admit.

"I imagine you do."

We've made no claim on each other, never spoken of our

emotions, never addressed the possibility that this was anything more than a flirtation. I don't even know what we want it to be. When Harry met me, when we started this, he knew I was engaged to marry another man. What can he possibly say about it now? But I know him well enough at this point—his body, his mannerisms, the tone of his voice—to know that he's unhappy with me. That after his announcement regarding the life insurance policy he expected me to call the whole thing off.

But there's an edge inside each of us, finely honed from a lifetime of making our own way in the world, from mistrusting others, from, at times, having to be a little bit ruthless. There are walls inside of us that are too impenetrable for this moment in time.

So instead, he says—

"Do you need me to help you relax?"

In a tone that is all too familiar, even if I can hear the meaning beneath the words, the sentiment he won't dare to say—

Do you need me?

"What did we say about terrible lines?" I tease, past the lump growing in my throat.

Yes.

"Come on. At this point, I think they're part of my charm."

"Maybe you're right. I finished packing." My gaze sweeps around the room. "I see you haven't started yet."

He shrugs, the sheet shifting down a bit, displaying an interesting amount of skin. "I figure I'll get to it when I can."

"Tonight will be busy with the captain's dinner and the ball," I reply.

"Not to mention your wedding."

I've seen Harry's derision directed at other guests onboard, the sharpness with which he can wield his words, his opinions, his cutting humor. But I've never been the recipient of them— not like this. And I feel each one dig a little deeper inside me, accepting the bitterness he throws at me as penance for the fact that I cannot—will not—trust him with the truth.

"I don't want to talk about Raymond. Not anymore. I'm here now," I whisper, leaning forward and brushing my lips against his.

He doesn't kiss me back like he normally does, and I can feel his anger, his frustration, and in return I give him all that is in my heart, all the things I cannot say with words, all the passion left inside me.

This final night of the cruise is the Captain's Ball, and as it is a masquerade, many of the guests have chosen to eschew their formal wear for flamboyant costumes. I opted for a simple demi mask to accompany the white gown Raymond purchased as my wedding dress. I figure I'll burn the dress when this is all over.

The silky material feels like insects crawling on my skin when it rubs against me, my heart pounding, my stomach raw.

I try to tell myself that this is just another role I am playing, that I am about to give the performance of a lifetime and then this will all be over soon.

The crew has adorned the grand ballroom with balloons and passed out paper hats to many of the guests so that we may ring in the last night of the cruise. It certainly feels momentous in a way—an end to the fantasy we have all lived at sea and a return to the realities and struggles of daily life.

At the same time, there's an undercurrent of sadness in the celebration. I recognize it on the faces of many of the guests, a maudlin emotion at the end of this chapter in their lives, even if it was a short one. Couples who met onboard the *Morro Castle* cling to each other, and I can't help but wonder what will come of their shipboard romances once they return home. If they live close together, perhaps they will be able to maintain the relationship, but really, what are the odds that a vacation romance lasts?

Will I see Harry again after this evening?

Raymond rises as I approach the table, but his presence barely registers as I glance down at the table and stop in my tracks.

Harry is seated next to my empty chair.

Of all the nights for him to come to dinner.

I focus on the place setting before me, unable to meet Harry's gaze beside me, unable to hide all the emotions churning inside me.

"You look beautiful," Harry whispers, his voice low enough for my ears alone.

"Don't," I hiss back. "Please, just don't."

What if Elena doesn't show up tonight? What if Harry's presence here complicates everything?

Just as the staff is serving the first course, the conversation lively at the table as the guests regale each other with stories of their cruise, a woman enters the grand ballroom.

My breath hitches.

She's alive.

Even from a distance, she's striking, her blue evening gown daring, her dark hair coiled atop her head, a black mask her only nod to the evening's festivities. She walks with purpose, wending her way through the room, her lips a bright red color.

She draws stares from more than a few sections of the room.

On the other side of me at the table, Raymond stiffens, his gaze on the woman in the blue dress.

I watch with a sort of detached, bemused fascination as the blood simply drains from his face.

"She's certainly striking," I murmur, realizing Raymond's unusual reaction has drawn some attention our way, Harry's gaze darting between me and the woman. "Is she someone you know?" I ask my fiancé.

The woman turns, and she makes eye contact with me for a split second, all the things that must go unsaid passing between us in a moment, before her gaze drifts to Raymond, a smile playing on her red-painted lips as though she's been waiting to see him for a very, very long time.

Raymond rises abruptly. "I'll be back," he says, barely affording me a glance before he leaves the dinner table.

My heart pounds.

I rise from my seat.

Harry stands as well.

"What's going on?" he asks me. "Who is that woman?"

Elena is nearly at the ballroom exit; Raymond strides behind her.

"I'll tell you later. I promise."

I need to be with Elena for this moment. She'll need my help with the last part of our plan.

"No. I saw the way he looked at that woman; his reaction—there's something going on here. Whatever it is, I'm coming with you."

Elena is almost at the doorway to the deck—

"Whatever is the matter?" Mrs. Gregory crows from her position on the other side of the table.

Harry mutters something unflattering under his breath, but neither one of us makes a move to answer her.

"I have to go," I hiss. "I'll explain everything to you later."

"Will you?" His gaze narrows. "Why do I have a hard time believing that?"

"I can't—"

There's a loud tapping noise on the microphone, a member of the cruise standing where the band normally is.

The crew member's voice shakes.

"Excuse me for the interruption. Unfortunately, I have some upsetting news to share with you all this evening. The captain is dead."

Pandemonium erupts in the ballroom, and in the chaos, Elena and Raymond are gone.

CHAPTER TWENTY-TWO

I dash after Raymond and Elena, heading toward the place on deck where we had planned for Elena to confront Raymond all those months ago when we used to pore over diagrams of the *Morro Castle*. Harry is hot on my heels.

After the commotion that erupted in the ballroom with the news of the captain's death, I lost sight of Raymond and Elena, all the plans we so carefully constructed shifting with the changing weather and the tragedy that has struck the ship as panic consumes the *Morro Castle*.

We head out onto the open deck, and I grab on to a railing as the ship sways, the weather that rolled in this morning only growing worse.

The seas slam against the ship, the wind whipping around us. There's a hurricane behind us and a nasty gale ahead of us, leaving us effectively trapped between the two. I've little experience with these types of storms, but given the vastness of the ocean and the relatively small size of the *Morro Castle* in comparison, it feels as though we are being tossed around like a tin can. What appeared to be a stalwart ship when we first boarded her nearly a week ago, now seems to face unfathomably difficult odds in nature's fury.

Not to mention the fact that the experienced captain is no longer at the helm.

All around me, the crew is rushing around, and the ship feels as though it is coming apart at the seams. There is a pitch to their voices that wasn't there before, and in their pinched faces, I see fear.

The captain's death has cast a pall over the remainder of the night, rumors spreading like wildfire throughout the ship that the man was poisoned.

The festivities come to a decisive end; the planned ball that was to take place after dinner abruptly cancelled, leaving many passengers adrift, costumed and searching for a source of revelry. I interacted with the captain little, but he seemed like a nice enough man.

I'm sure the rest of the crew is more than capable, but there's something unsettling about losing the man who was supposed to ferry us all home. Given the size of the ship and the weather conditions surrounding us, I can't imagine the pressure that the crew must feel in his absence as they attempt to steer us all to safety.

I must find Elena and Raymond.

Harry takes my hand, and we continue down the ship, searching for them.

The ship rocks again, jolting me, and my shoulder hits the wall, pain stabbing me.

"Are you alright?" Harry calls out, but I don't answer him, all my focus on getting to Elena.

There's a whiff of something in the air as we hurry down the deck.

"Do you smell something?" I ask Harry.

He shakes his head.

"It almost smells like smoke," I say, an unpleasant memory filling me. It's just like in the nightmare—

"Maybe one of the guests was smoking," Harry suggests.

"Maybe."

It doesn't smell like cigarette smoke, though—

It smells like a fire.

"Come on," Harry says, tugging me away from the crowd.

There's something in the air tonight, something that just feels *off*, and I can't shake the uneasy feeling in my stomach or the worry that fills me when I look around the deck.

The alcohol has been flowing freely for hours now, and no matter how hard the crew tries to stop the festivities, the crowd is like a freight train hurtling toward a destination it's long since fixed its sights on. But it's clear that whatever we're sailing into is dangerous; the weather is growing worse and worse with each minute that passes, the ship swaying and tilting in the rough seas.

Harry pulls me out of the way just as one of the other passengers hurries in front of me, nearly knocking me over, leaning their body over the rail and throwing up.

"The *Titanic* hit an iceberg," I murmur to myself. "No icebergs here."

"What did you say?" Harry asks.

"Just trying to reassure myself. It's a little hard not to think of maritime disasters now, to not feel like we're just a toy boat being tossed around by a giant, angry ocean."

"Why on earth would you think of the *Titanic* right now?"

"I'm trying *not* to think of the *Titanic*."

"Well, now I'm thinking about it." He stops, grabbing hold of the rail with one hand, his other wrapped around my waist, holding me close to him, keeping me in the curve of his embrace. He leans forward, his lips brushing against my ear. "It's okay. We'll be okay. This is a sturdy ship. No doubt, it was built to withstand things like this especially after what happened to the *Titanic*. We'll be fine."

We must be little more than a few hours away from reaching port in New York City. Hopefully, this will all be over soon.

I turn the corner, expecting to see Elena and Raymond where we agreed to meet, but instead the space is filled with the crew, running around in a panic.

The wail of a siren reverberates through the ship.

CHAPTER TWENTY-THREE

ELENA

Elena raises the pistol, pointing it at Raymond, his back to the railing. The boat rocks; the weather conditions have deteriorated considerably since they came out on deck.

So far nothing this evening has gone as she anticipated. The spot where she and Katie had planned to lure Raymond was filled with crew members rushing around to fill new posts after the captain's death.

So now she is all alone.

It's dangerous being out here on the open deck, the chance that someone might see them a concern. When they were planning this night, she and Katie decided that it would be best to get him as close to the railing as possible—it can't be an easy feat to push a man overboard, even one of average height and build like Raymond.

The wind whips around them, the mighty seas churning below and battering the side of the *Morro Castle*. The ship rocks a bit, Elena's legs unsteady beneath her. For as many times as she imagined this moment in her mind, she didn't account for the weather, for the possibility that they would be sailing between a nor'easter and a hurricane.

The weather is both an advantage and a threat—with the rain coming down, it obscures them from view more than normal, but at the same time, Elena isn't much of a shot under ideal conditions, and between the wind, and the rain, and the rocking of the boat, her body trembles.

Raymond reaches out, gripping the rail behind him for purchase, a flash of unease crossing his face.

Good, let him be the one who is unsettled now, the one who is scared. Let him have a taste of the fear that has plagued her for so long.

Seeing him again like this sends a flood of memories through her—of the first time they met when she was at lunch in the city, of their courtship when he was so romantic, and attentive, and she thought she'd met the man she would love for the rest of her life, of their wedding day, and then of all the struggles in their marriage, that fateful night when it all ended.

She swears she can smell the smoke from the fire that night.

The hand holding the gun isn't as steady as she'd like.

"I knew you were on the ship," Raymond says, breaking the silence between them, his words a shout over the wind, the rain slowly lessening.

"You don't want to do this." Raymond's voice is surprisingly calm despite the barrel of the gun pointed at him.

That he thinks he has any hope of swaying her from her course is almost laughable considering all she's been through. He has no idea who rose from the ashes of the fire he set.

"I trusted you," Elena says. "I'm not the only woman who made that mistake, am I?"

She waits to see if he will plead for his life, if he will argue with her, try to convince her that he never meant to hurt her, that she is mistaken, that all those things that happened to her in the house in New York City were mere accidents. She waits to see if he will lie to her as he once did so easily.

Raymond's expression is blank, but it's no matter.

The words aren't for him. They're for her.

It feels good to speak now, to make him listen to her. It feels good to be the one with the power after feeling powerless for so long. It was one thing to know it in her heart, but another entirely to see it with her eyes. For so long, she doubted her own instincts, her memories, her thoughts. At times, in that big house, she wondered if she was hallucinating all the misfortunes befalling her, if the accidents were a product of an overactive imagination as Raymond suggested.

She didn't realize back then that the threat he posed wasn't just to her physical safety, but to her spirit and her soul. She may have escaped his physical clutches, but every other part of her has been affected as well, and it is those months of doubting herself that make her the angriest.

Now that she has this moment, his undivided attention, she wants to revel in it, wants to make him feel every ounce of pain that she has suffered. "Do you have nothing to say to me?"

Maybe he realizes the futility in such an attempt given the conviction in her gaze, or he simply doesn't care anymore, but he remains silent. Regardless, it is as though the mask has been dropped and now she sees definitively that the man she thought she loved never existed at all. It's surprising how much it matters; the difference between knowing something in her heart and seeing it with her very eyes.

"You knew what I had been through, that I had lost my parents, that I was alone in the world. You knew how desperately I believed in you."

"Perhaps that was your mistake," he scoffs.

Was it? Was it her mistake to believe that he was a good man, to hope for happiness in her future, that at last she would have the family that was denied to her when her parents died? For a long time, she believed that lie, blamed herself for falling victim to Raymond's advances, didn't trust herself for the fact that she didn't see what was wrong in her marriage, didn't realize all along that Raymond sought to deceive her. But now she knows better. Now she sees that the only person here to blame is him.

"There were others weren't there?" she asks. "Others besides me?"

"I'm not going to answer that."

Of course he won't. There's no accountability with him, no remorse.

"You were clever to make everything look like it was an accident, to make me doubt myself."

"How did you survive the fire?"

She smiles. "That must have frustrated you once you realized I was still alive. Knowing I bested you. The staff helped me. You see, I made friends with them when I was in that house. I got to know them. They protected me."

"Where's the money?" he asks.

"What money? My money? My father worked hard for my inheritance, wanted me to have it in the event of his death. I wasn't going to let you steal my legacy, too. I knew you would have to go down to Cuba to get the money. It was only a matter of time."

"Is it on this ship?"

"Do you really think I would make a mistake like that? It's somewhere you will never get it."

"And Ava, you came for her, too, didn't you?"

She doesn't deny it. Her daughter and her future, her safety, has been the only thing keeping her going for so long now.

His eyes narrow. "How did you know I would be on this ship?"

"Like I said, you really should have paid more attention to the staff."

She sees the moment when it comes to him, all the pieces

tumbling together. He's always been a smart one, and a cunning adversary, too.

"That little maid you had."

"Katie? Yes. Of course, you know her better as Catherine."

"I knew there was something familiar about her . . . I thought it was because I had seen her at some function or another."

"Oh, if only you knew how much we worried about that. Even with her changing her hair color, she was concerned you would recognize her. After all, she worked in your household for a year. But I had a feeling you wouldn't. You were always good at ignoring people you thought were beneath you."

Anger flashes across his face, and she remembers, too, how much he always hated being corrected, how desperately he always needed to be right.

"You had her attacked on the deck on the first night here," Elena says.

"It wasn't supposed to be the first night," he replies as though that is the salient point. "The man I hired screwed up. And then he disappeared."

"I thought you had to marry women in order to take their money."

She and Katie had talked about it at length, Elena's greatest fear, the dangerous flaw in the plan being the possibility that it would put Katie's life in jeopardy—or Ava's. They had consoled themselves with the belief that if Katie and Raymond weren't married, Raymond wouldn't be able to access Katie's supposed fortune, and that a prolonged engagement would keep her safe.

"Not always. Sometimes, yes. In Catherine's case, I took out a life insurance policy. Hedging my bets."

It's the most candid he's been since they started this conversation, and Elena can't help but think it's because she's outsmarted him, and he wants her to know that in some things he still has the upper hand.

Her eyes water, the smell of smoke assailing her again. Her legs tremble beneath her. In the beginning after the fire, she had attacks throughout the day, memories when the fire would come rushing back to her, pulling her out of wherever she was and sucking her back into the past and that horrible night.

It can't be happening again now.

Raymond gestures toward the gun in her hand. "You've had your say. You have the money. You can go on with the rest of your life. Put the gun down."

She laughs. Who was the version of herself that he knew? Was she once so young and naïve that he believed he could manipulate her so easily?

"Do you really think I'm that stupid? That I believe you'll just let all of this go?"

"So, you mean to shoot me? I don't think so. You haven't the stomach to take a life."

"Ordinarily, I'd agree with you, but in this case, I'll just think of all the women I'm saving. Besides, there's nothing I wouldn't do to keep my daughter safe."

"She's my daughter, too."

It's a statement of fact and a threat all rolled into one, and she knows without a doubt that if Raymond is alive, she and her daughter will never know peace. He will do anything to protect himself and she will always be a loose end, the person who has unmasked him, the person who can reveal his true nature to the world.

Her finger moves to the trigger.

Raymond rushes at her, fury in his eyes, and she squeezes the trigger, the recoil from the gun jerking against her body.

Raymond's eyes go slack with shock as a red stain spreads over the center of his white evening shirt.

For a moment, she can do little more than stare at that stain, and then she charges at him with a strength and fury she didn't know she possessed, and there's a crack, wood splintering as his body hits the rail, and then she watches as it tumbles over the edge of the ship, leaving her holding the intact railing staring down at the dark sea, wondering if she managed to kill him.

CHAPTER TWENTY-FOUR

CATHERINE

We climb the stairs, searching for Elena and Raymond, a commotion sounding on A deck outside near the ship's stern.

I tug at the bodice of my dress, warmth filling me the higher we climb.

I push the door leading outside open and pull my hand back, the wood surprisingly hot beneath my touch.

"What—"

I can do little more than gape at the scene in front of me—the middle of the ship is on fire, the deck ablaze. Through some of the other doorways on deck, groups of people stream out of their cabins, coughing loudly, the acrid smell of smoke sticking to their clothes. Some are still wearing their pajamas, others taking the time to throw a coat on over their sleepwear.

How many people were asleep when the fire broke out? How many cabins has the fire reached?

No one is attempting to put the fire out, and I instinctively look for something—only to realize the futility of such an action. A blaze of this magnitude . . . but surely, they have hoses aboard the ship?

A man runs by us, blood trickling down the side of his face, a nasty gash on his head.

"Sir, do you need medical assistance?" I call out.

"I'm looking for my son," he shouts, hurrying down the deck toward the fire.

All around us, people scream and cry, searching for loved ones, some like the man sporting various injuries no doubt in their attempt to escape the fire. I search for the familiar uniforms of the crew, hoping they can bring some order to this business, tell us what we need to do, what the proper protocol is for a situation such as this one.

Will they be able to get the fire under control?

Why isn't anyone trying to?

I don't realize I've spoken the last words aloud until Harry answers me.

"The man next to me said they tried. There was a problem with the hoses. They didn't work."

"What does that mean for all of us?"

He doesn't answer me.

Are we going to have to abandon the ship? I rush over to

the railing, terror filling me at the sight of the bottomless water. The seas look rough, the storms surrounding us battering the ship. Considering how much the *Morro Castle* is affected in such weather, it's daunting to imagine how one of the tiny rescue vessels will fare in such harsh conditions.

Off in the distance, one of the lifeboats has already launched into the water, and as the moonlight shifts, it illuminates the white uniforms of the crew seated aboard the boat.

A ship of this size and experience—surely there's a plan in place to evacuate all of us safely in the event of a fire.

I spy a crew member up ahead of us on deck, but he hurries past the passengers calling out to him for help, a life jacket on over his uniform as he rushes past women and children without preservers.

Suddenly, it is abundantly clear that no one is coming to help us, and if we are to be saved, then we must save ourselves.

I grip Harry's arm, grateful that I am not alone in this. "We should go back through the corridors and try to wake people up. Help them get out."

A man standing near to me shakes his head, tears in his eyes. "There's no point in going back through the corridor on this deck. You can't. The fire has already overtaken it. We were one of the last ones out."

"And everyone else?" I ask.

"I hope they made it," he replies.

Where is Elena? And Ava?

"Stay here." Harry tells me.

"What? No. I'm not leaving you."

"We need life jackets to be safe. Let me see if I can find some."

"You heard what the man said—the corridor has been over-taken by the fire."

"I'll try one of the other hallways. They might be passable. We need life jackets. I'll knock on doors as well to warn any others. Wait for me here. It's too dangerous for both of us to go."

I want to argue with him, want to demand that I come, too, but he's already turned away from me and gone before the words escape my throat. I move to follow him when someone bumps into me.

"Catherine," a woman shouts, grabbing my arms.

"Emily! Ava!"

Tears fill Emily's eyes, and I get the sense that she is barely holding it all together, Ava in her arms.

"Where is her father?" Emily asks.

"I don't know. We need to get off the ship—the fire is rag-ing out of control."

"We tried to get one of the lifeboats, but it was filled with the crew," Emily answers.

"I know. A friend of mine went to try to get some life vests. They might be our best bet at this point."

Emily takes my hand, and we walk down the deck together, Ava's arms wrapped around Emily's neck.

The farther we walk, the thicker the smoke grows, the wind blowing it toward us. I cover my mouth just as Emily does to

Ava's and hers, but it does little to stave off the coughing that rattles my chest, the acrid smell burning my eyes until they water.

The memory it conjures is a horrible one—that night with Elena, I was convinced we would die. The fire seemed insurmountable, but when I saw how hard it was for Elena to walk, how badly Raymond had drugged her with the hope that she wouldn't escape, it renewed my resolve. I couldn't let her die in that house.

But now, facing this fire, stuck on a ship in the middle of the ocean—

I pray that Harry is alright, but it's hard to have much faith considering the conditions on the open deck. If it's like this out here, how bad must it be inside the hallways and rooms of the ship?

Where is Elena?

The ship is large enough that there are plenty of places she can be, not to mention the fact that perhaps other lifeboats have launched, and she could be on one of those headed toward safety.

And Raymond?

I hope he's at the bottom of the sea.

Up ahead, I spy one of the lifeboats lowering into the water.

"Wait," I yell, pushing my way to the front, pulling Emily with me.

I turn, ushering Emily and Ava forward.

"Take her. There are two empty seats. It's your best chance."

"Are you sure?" Emily asks. "I—"

I nod.

"We have to go," one of the crew members shouts from the lifeboat.

I watch as Emily and Ava climb into the boat, as it's lowered into the dark water.

I turn away, heading toward the spot where I last saw Harry, where he asked me to wait for him. He's nowhere to be seen on the deck, the panic spreading as though everyone else has now realized that there is no hope of putting the fire out, the wind feeding its growth at a frightening rate, and as quickly as it is moving through the ship, we have little choice but to abandon the *Morro Castle*.

Cries flood the deck, hysteria building among the passengers. Everyone is looking to others to help, for someone to lead, to tell us what to do, but no one is assuming such a role, exacerbating the fear spreading across the ship nearly as quickly as the fire.

And then I see Harry, walking toward me, one life preserver in hand.

I throw my arms around him, and he holds on to me tightly, coughing as we embrace.

"I was so worried you wouldn't come back," I say.

"I worried myself a time or two, if I'm being honest. It's bad down there. Can you swim?" he asks me, his voice grim.

"No, I never learned. Not much occasion for swimming in New York City," I say, struggling and failing to add some levity to the situation, my voice trembling with each word that falls from my lips.

I've never been so scared in all my life.

After the fateful day in New York, I had some dreams of the fire, but each time when I woke up, I calmed myself down with the reminder that as horrible as it had been, we'd survived, and all my focus was dedicated to our plan to stop Raymond from hurting another woman, of rescuing Ava.

But this? I don't know how we can survive conditions like these.

"I found Ava, Elena's daughter. She was able to get on a lifeboat with her nanny."

"Why didn't you join them?"

"There wasn't room."

"Put this on." Harry hands me the life jacket. His hands shake as he fastens it around my body.

"What about you?" I ask. "Were you only able to find the one?"

"I gave one to a woman who needed it. I kept this one for you."

"What about you? Can you swim?"

"I can. Never in conditions like this, though."

"Do you really think the lifeboats can save us?" I ask him.

"It's our best shot. Hopefully, the crew has been able to send an SOS and nearby ships will come to our aid. These are hardly ideal conditions for a lifeboat, but maybe we won't be in the water for too long if there's a ship close enough to rescue us."

"Surely, a vessel this size and a fire this size will have caught someone's notice."

"Let's hope so."

Panic seems to have settled in around us, the passengers ill-equipped to navigate the fire. There was no drill, no practice for us on what to do in the event of such a catastrophe, and in the face of the immense danger before us, it is difficult to process all the surrounding threats, to decide what is best to do.

The crew seems equally unprepared for such a calamity, their faces slack with shock. Just a few nights ago at dinner, I'd heard the captain proclaim to Raymond that he had the utmost confidence in his ship, that her sturdiness was uncontested. It's difficult to believe such things now.

The engines have stopped. We're no longer heading toward New York, but instead are listing from side to side in the middle of the sea.

A scream rises in my throat, panic building.

A few steps away from us, a priest has gathered a crowd in prayer.

Smoke billows around us.

"Some of the lifeboats have burned," Harry says, his voice grim as he surveys the deck. Whatever the conditions were like indoors, the ones outside have deteriorated considerably since he went to get our life jackets.

He's right—some of the boats have caught fire. Others are

drifting in the ocean with just a few people in them, most filled with crew.

"Not a woman or child in sight," Harry says in disgust, his gaze on the uniformed crew floating to safety, empty seats surrounding them.

Beside me, a woman walks over to the railing, her gaze trained to the water.

I open my mouth to say something—anything—but she's already climbing the railing before I can get the words out.

She jumps, her body hitting the water moments later. Farther down on the deck, others join her, deciding their best odds are with the sea rather than remaining with the burning ship.

I glance around, searching for a lifeboat, searching for—

"They've only been able to release about half of them," Harry says. "There aren't nearly enough lifeboats for all of us. The crew is almost gone. We're all alone now."

The deck is growing unbearably hot beneath my feet, burning through the soles of my shoes.

A curse falls from my lips. "We're going to have to jump, aren't we?"

"Yes."

"From this height, the water—"

It's impossible to miss the fact that some of the bodies jumping over the railing are hitting the water with sickening smacks.

"We could break a limb—or our necks—yes."

So, we take our chances with either the fire or the water. Given the intensity of the raging inferno, the smoke billowing, it's not much of a choice. At least, the life jacket will keep me from drowning, or so I hope, although the idea of hurtling my body into that water knowing that I cannot swim terrifies me.

"Watch out for the propeller," Harry instructs. "When we jump, we need to make sure we're clear of the ship."

It's windy out on deck—how much will that alter the trajectory of where we land?

I reach out to pull on the life jacket so that it will inflate before I jump. The idea of being stuck in the water, unable to swim—

"Wait," Harry shouts. "Don't inflate it yet. From this height, you'll break your neck when you hit the water."

"I can't swim," I hiss through gritted teeth.

"You'll be fine. Just inflate it as soon as you hit the water. Trust me."

Harry leans over, hooking an arm around my waist and pulling me toward him, his mouth coming down on mine in a fierce kiss. It feels a bit like what it might be—a goodbye—and tears prick my eyes.

What could have happened between us if we'd just had a little more time? If we'd met under different circumstances?

Harry releases me slowly, his gaze locked on mine, and for

the first time, I'm seeing a side of him I've never witnessed before, a vulnerability I've only caught glimpses of.

I lift my hand and cup his cheek, words failing me.

And then it's over, and we both turn toward the railing, and it belatedly occurs to me that we're standing near the spot where the man tumbled overboard that first night, and now we're the ones about to hurl our bodies into the water.

I hesitate, staring down at the ocean beneath me, my fingers gripping the metal railing.

"It will be alright," Harry shouts from his position next to me, but it's impossible to believe him when his voice is devoid of its characteristic charm, the smoothness shaky at best.

He's as scared as I am.

I close my eyes, and then I'm jumping, as far out from the *Morro Castle* as I can manage, my body suspended in air for a string of breathless moments when I wonder if this is death, or somewhere in between, and then I hit the ice-cold water with a sharp, burning pain piercing my body.

CHAPTER TWENTY-FIVE

ELENA

When her body hits the water, it's the cold that surprises her the most. She spent her whole life hurtling her body into the sea, jumping over the waves, diving down into the ocean's depths, but that was nothing like this. This sea is unforgiving and brutal, the waves pounding her body like a piece of driftwood, water filling her mouth, her nostrils. All around her, she hears the screams of those who weren't so lucky to hit the water intact, those who were injured by the impact or by the life jackets they were wearing. She reaches out to offer a hand to someone in need, but she comes up empty, the ocean slipping through her fingers until she realizes she is really and truly alone, the nearest survivor somewhere unseen in the inky black water.

She yells for Ava until her voice becomes hoarse with the effort, until her cheeks are stained with tears.

No one calls back to her.

They're out there somewhere—the sounds of groups of people screaming and crying audible in the distance.

There were no life jackets, but for someone who lived her life in the sea that was hardly the most daunting part of the endeavor, what she left back on the *Morro Castle* far more terrifying.

She prays her daughter is safe. Surely, they would have evacuated the children into lifeboats first. She prays her daughter is waiting for her on the shore.

Elena reaches out and her hand brushes against something—someone. She opens her mouth to speak, but as the current pushes the body toward her—

It's a woman.

She floats lifelessly in the water, her life jacket keeping her from sinking.

A scream builds in Elena's throat, terror filling her.

It's bitterly cold in the water, the waves knocking her body around.

Her cries join that of the others, spread around the burning carcass of the *Morro Castle,* searching for family and friends.

She must swim. She must try.

The strokes come as naturally to her as breathing, the familiar rhythm of it all kicking into gear as she realizes she has two choices: she can die here, or she can take her chances and face the threat of dying as she searches for the shore.

Her blue dress sticks to her body with each kick, each pull, the conditions in the water and the rough waves more treacherous than any she's used to.

She doesn't know how long she swims for, her mind sharpened to no more than the rhythm of her strokes, the incessant burning in her lungs, the ache in her limbs. The shore feels far away now, the difficulty of the journey before her hitting with the unmistakable sensation that somehow her destination is slipping further from her grasp.

It seemed possible when she was standing on the ship, memories of Havana waters in her mind, but this is something entirely different, something she didn't account for.

The waves are nearly unbearable, the storm around her churning up the angry seas. For all the times she's swum in the ocean before, she's never been in conditions like this. Despite her best efforts, the seawater fills her mouth, forcing a bracing cough from her chest and then another.

Elena stops, treading water as the waves roll over her, turning and glancing behind her to orient herself, to get a glimpse of the mighty ship. Many of its glittering lights have gone out, but it's still there, off in the horizon, the fire raging. She's too far away to see if any people are on the decks, a few lifeboats illuminated by the light coming off the ship.

The urge to make the sign of the cross overwhelms her, the desire to pray for her fellow passengers.

Is Ava alive?

Katie?

Raymond?

Off in the distance, she can see the lights from the shore.

Elena kicks even harder.

CHAPTER TWENTY-SIX

CATHERINE

My life has been bifurcated into two parts—before my body hit the water that horrible night and after—when I floated in the ocean awaiting rescue for hours, doing my best to swim to shore to no avail, until finally a fishing boat piloted by locals came and rescued me, hauling my cold, waterlogged, and weary body aboard their crowded vessel.

There were others like me, and we huddled together, wearing matching expressions of shock. There were no words, just horror. I scanned the faces of my fellow passengers, searching for Elena and Harry, but they were nowhere to be seen. I opened my mouth to ask if anyone knew them, but the futility of such a question considering the vastness of the ocean and the chaos of the night hit me in that moment, and I said nothing, my grief overwhelming me.

At least Ava got a lifeboat out.

All around me, the others wore that same dejected expression in their eyes; no doubt for many, their loss was far greater than mine: children, spouses, parents, the list never-ending.

How did such a thing happen? How were we the survivors?

They took us to be examined by doctors and nurses, a makeshift staging area that had been organized to assist the passengers of the *Morro Castle*. Twice, I asked where I was, and twice they told me the name of the little town in New Jersey, but each time the answer they gave me slipped through my fingers, my memory clouded by everything that had happened, the lack of sleep catching up to me, the effects of the cold water leaving my body exhausted.

There was one moment that was crystal clear: that sensation of me jumping off the ship, that moment when I felt as though I hovered between salvation and death before my body hit the water. I never asked Elena what it was like for her in the fire, if she felt as though she had faced death and then walked away from it, but the sea was a bit like that for me—it was unmistakable how close I'd come, and I was uncomfortably aware of the fact that it could have gone either way, that I was one of the lucky ones when so many others weren't.

I kept waiting for Elena or Harry to show up at the medical tent; I even feared that Raymond would, but none of them ever did. I asked after Ava and one of the nurses wrote her name down on a notepad along with the other children who had been missing or separated from their families. After all our planning, revenge so close we could taste it, everything changed in the fire.

One of the nurses told me that there were reports of survivors turning up all along the Jersey shore, the ocean's swells and the rescue boats carrying us to distant places. There was little more to do than pray that Elena and Harry had made it and were at the same moment as me lying in cots along the Jersey shore receiving medical care, that Ava was safe.

When it became apparent that my injuries were superficial and nothing a little rest and fluids couldn't cure, I was released, many of the others in far greater need than I was.

There was only one place I could think to go—

I had to see the *Morro Castle* one last time.

I've never been to Asbury Park before, but by all accounts, it has served as a vacation destination for all looking for sun, sand, and fun for a few days. Today, it certainly lives up to its reputation despite the macabre events of the last twenty-four hours.

The beach and boardwalk are crowded with onlookers—thousands, maybe—some fully dressed, others in bathing attire—staring out at the charred remains of the *Morro Castle*. One of the rescue ships tried to tow the ship in the water to bring it to shore, but the tie between the two broke in the process, and the *Morro Castle* became beached near the Jersey shore.

Vendors sell food on the boardwalk, and the sweet and salty scents send my stomach roiling. Children run around, their parents gawking at the sight before them, the mighty ship beached in Asbury Park, New Jersey, its heft stabilized by cables anchoring it to the ground. Its gleaming black and white appearance is now a burnt husk before us.

For a moment, I think I'm going to be sick.

Tourists pose in front of the ship to have their photographs taken. They climb into lifeboats that should have been our salvation and have washed ashore, now dotting the beach surrounding the *Morro Castle*. Will these images hang on walls in their homes, sit in frames, or merely be used to show friends and family, regaling them with stories of the demise of the mighty *Morro Castle*?

What is it that brings people to a sight such as this? Is it some desire to face a nightmare or to see something horrible that has happened to others and take comfort in the fact that it wasn't them on the ship? Or are they merely here to pay their respects, to honor the dead and aid the survivors?

I suppose the increased attention will help the town; with the Depression, everyone is struggling so much, and the townspeople have been generous and kind to the survivors, offering us clothes, shelter, and food while we wait for more assistance to come.

I walk by a group eyeing me with curiosity, and as I pass them by, I hear their whispers—

Do you think—Do you think she was on the ship?

I certainly look like it in my borrowed dress, my elegant gowns likely charred somewhere in the ship's bowels. I can feel the weight of their gaze on my retreating back, and I wish to tell them the truth, to satisfy their prurient curiosity—

However bad they imagine it was, the reality of experiencing it was far worse.

The sight of the ship is staggering, the destruction the fire wrought undeniably stark before me. Smoke billows from the *Morro Castle* still. Mangled lifeboats hang from the side of the boat, tilting listlessly, and I can't help but wonder about the people who could have been saved but weren't, all those poor souls lost at sea. I can hear the screams of the people jumping to their deaths, the smack of their bodies hitting the propeller, the cries of the survivors in the water, desperate for assistance. And then there are the silent ones that I wonder about, the ones who fell asleep in their staterooms thinking that they would awake to see the ship docked in New York, that they would be reunited with their families, the ones who burned to death while they slept. Those poor, poor souls.

Dead bodies lie on the beach, covered in blankets and sheets in an attempt to preserve some dignity in their final repose.

I shudder.

I wrap my arms around my waist and walk in the sand,

scanning the deceased, fearing that I will see someone I recognize. Some family members will have bodies to bury, but so many others won't even have that. Their loved ones lie somewhere in the depths of the ocean, never to be found.

I doubt anyone who has seen this sight will ever forget it in all their lives. I know I never will.

"Miss. Miss."

I turn at the sound of the voice and stare into the lens of a camera.

"Could you take our picture?" the man connected to the camera asks me, gesturing toward the woman and children standing behind him. "In front of the ship?"

Wordlessly, I take the camera from him, snapping a photograph as he asked, the sight of that ship in the background a hulking menace.

I hand the camera back to him, and I can't resist asking—

"Do you know where the medical tents are? Where they're keeping the survivors? I'm looking for my friends."

I'm nearly exhausted by the time I reach the makeshift medical center, belatedly realizing that I should have let them administer aid to me longer, that being out here in the bright sun with all the loud sounds and strange smells was too much for me. In this moment, I yearn for the comfort of a hotel room, even the worn sheets of the cramped room I called home before I moved into better quarters while I played the role of young heiress. And still, the desire to know what happened to the others is overwhelming, spurring me on.

I search the patients, my gaze sweeping over the tent. Some of them are seated upright in bed, their limbs wrapped with white gauze, pain etched on their faces. Others look to be unconscious as they lie in their medical cots.

"Excuse me."

I step out of the way in time for a pair of orderlies to pass me by.

They're carrying a body on a stretcher, a white sheet draped over it.

I know what those white sheets mean.

There's a nurse standing off to the side by a few beds, a clipboard in her hand. One of the doctors asks her a question, and by the way she answers him, the natural authority in her voice, it's clear she is well-informed.

I hurry over to her.

"Ma'am, I'm sorry to bother you, but I was on the *Morro Castle*—"

Sympathy fills her gaze.

"—And I'm looking for some of my friends." I hesitate. "And my fiancé, and his daughter, and her nanny. Is there a list of the passengers you've treated? Or a manifest of the missing and accounted for?"

"We've written down the names of the ones who came in here lucid or had some identification on them that we could use. There weren't many of those, unfortunately. As for a broader list, hopefully, we'll be able to gather something more comprehensive in a few days' time. Right now, my understanding is that many are missing and unaccounted for. We aren't the only place the wounded are going, so it will take some time to coordinate with everyone. I can go over the list of the names I do have, though." Her expression softens, her voice unbearably kind. "My condolences for everything you've been through."

Tears fill my eyes. "Thank you."

I give her the names, holding my breath while she checks the list she has.

She shakes her head. "They're not on our list. Like I said, it's possible they were here, but we couldn't identify them. Or they could have ended up elsewhere."

She doesn't say the rest, but I can tell from her expression that what goes unsaid is—

They might've died somewhere in the sea.

Tears well in her eyes. "It's a terrible thing, what you all have been through."

"It is," I whisper. I will leave here and I will go find a place to sleep, and I will fall apart completely.

"I'll give you a moment," the nurse adds. "I need to administer some medication to my patients, but if you have any other questions, I'll be happy to answer them."

"Thank you. For everything. For caring for so many of us. It means a great deal."

She leaves me alone, and I sit down in an empty chair, my legs nearly giving out beneath me.

I wish we had never been on that ship to begin with.

Was it sabotage? Or arson? Or a simple accident, even a foreseeable one?

There have been whispers in the medical tents, speculation on deck during the panic.

I've no doubt that there will be plenty of blame and finger-pointing to go around once this whole business is finished. Certainly, there are many places where it seems as though this tragedy could have been averted. All I can pray is that something like this never happens again and no one else must know the horrors we went through.

I rise from the seat, searching for the nurse to give her one last thanks, but she's busy with her patients, and they clearly need her more than I do.

I pray they make it through the night.

As I turn away from the medical center, struggling to keep it all together, all I can think is:

Am I the only one who survived?

"Miss?" the nurse shouts behind me.

I turn.

"I'm sorry, she wasn't on the list, but there's a woman here who says she has an Ava Warner in her care."

CHAPTER TWENTY-SEVEN

A week after the fire on the *Morro Castle,* a parcel is delivered to me at the Plaza Hotel in New York City, my new digs courtesy of the engagement ring I pawned to pay for rooms for me and Ava and her nanny, and to provide for Emily's salary until Ava's future is settled. Despite Raymond's penchant for fake jewelry, at least my ring was blessedly real. I don't know where the diamond came from or how he came by it, or how many women's fingers it adorned before mine, but I'm grateful for it just the same.

Jewelry is often a powerful currency when we have so little else.

I take the parcel, studying my name that is written on the outside in unfamiliar writing.

I open it carefully, looking for clues as to who might have possibly sent it to me.

My fingers freeze as I remove the item from the packaging, a familiar cover staring back at me.

A cry escapes my lips.

The Thin Man.

My heart pounds as I examine the book, a piece of paper staring out at me from the middle of the novel.

It's not my copy, of course, mine is likely at the bottom of the Atlantic Ocean, but the sight of it sends a thrill through me, my lips curving into a smile.

I unfold the piece of paper, studying the words there, my smile widening.

In case you want to see how it ends. I'm staying at the Biltmore. Harry

I sink down on the bed, relief filling me as I clutch the novel to my chest. I'm not surprised that he was able to find me considering how many connections he has and how utterly charming he can be. And somehow, for a man who could have easily given me diamonds, he found the perfect gift for me, and at the same time, I cannot think of anything that is more Harry than making me go to him when he just as easily could have come to me.

Insufferable man.

He's alive.

I grab my coat.

The man at the front desk gives me Harry's room number and says he is expecting me, and as I ride the elevator up to his floor, watching the numbers tick by, I try to decide whether his confidence in us, as if we are a foregone conclusion, is charming or annoying. Funny, how the two traits can live on a knife's edge of each other.

When I step off the elevator, I've nearly worked out in my mind what I want and how I'm going to get it, because for me, some things are foregone conclusions, too.

I knock on the front door of Harry's suite, a sliver of nerves filling me. That last night on the *Morro Castle* was so chaotic that we never had a chance to speak of our feelings or desires. I *think* I know how he feels and what he wants—or what he could want if he was only shown the way—but the fear is still there. When you're pretending to be someone else, then it's easy to tell yourself that if you aren't wanted, it's fine because it isn't *you* that they're rejecting, just someone you're pretending to be. But with Harry it's different, because I feel as though I have stripped myself bare before him, both literally and figuratively, and I've let him see pieces of myself that I haven't shared with others. And after the *Morro Castle*, well, I don't think I'll ever be the same person I was. How can you go through a thing like that and not come out of it as someone changed?

The door opens.

Harry stands on the other side of the threshold.

For a moment, I consider saying something clever, returning his flirtation with some of my own, but all I can do is walk into his arms, basking in the familiar scent of his cologne, the feel of his body against mine.

He runs his fingers through my hair, his mouth finding mine. Tears trickle down my cheeks, all the events of the past few weeks catching up to me.

We come together in a rush, fumbling with each other's clothes, our bodies hitting the bed before we're able to get our shoes off.

There's desperation in our joining, this need to feel alive after all we've been through, a desire to find a moment of joy in a sea of unspeakable grief.

We lie together on the bed, our bodies beside each other, our fingers intertwined.

"Are you ready to tell me about it? About that woman in the ballroom—and how you found yourself engaged to a man I know you never wished to marry?" he asks me.

I nod. "I'm sorry I didn't tell you earlier."

"I thought about it for a long time after the fire on the *Morro Castle*. You worked for her, didn't you? She was the employer you told me about. The one who was like a friend to you."

"Yes."

"I don't understand, though. If you used to work in the house—how did you pose as his fiancée without Raymond recognizing you?"

"I told you—my hair used to be red. Some dye, makeup, the right clothes, the right costume jewels, and suddenly, I was no longer the invisible maid he never paid attention to but someone who became worthy of his time." I shrug. "I always wanted to be an actress. It wasn't all that different from playing a role before an audience of one. It helped that Elena was able to give me some advice on how to appeal to Raymond and how to handle him, on how to behave like a real-life heiress."

"And after hearing about her experiences, you decided you needed to get even closer to him, to risk your life as well?"

"I saw what he did to her in that house, the hell that she lived through. After what you told me about your father and what he did to your mother, I would think you more than anyone would understand that need for justice, the desire to see him pay for the harm he'd caused."

Understanding flashes in his eyes.

"I was able to help, and after all Elena had done for me, taking me in after my mother died, it felt like the right thing to do."

"I don't understand why you had to become engaged to him in order to get your revenge."

"Because we needed someone who would be close to him. Someone who could keep an eye on things. There's a child. Elena's daughter, Ava. She survived the fire. She and her nanny are staying at the hotel in the room next to mine. Given all that Raymond is capable of, the way he treated Ava in the past, we didn't trust that he wouldn't do something to her, too."

"The whole time you knew how dangerous he was. Why put yourself at risk?"

"It wasn't just Elena. There were others before her. Wealthy women he conned in one way or another. He'd hurt so many people. He deserved to pay for what he had done before another woman suffered. We talked about going to the police, but Raymond was so smart, so careful. One time, Elena was suspicious of some of the 'accidents' that were befalling her in the house. He told her that she was overwrought, that he was worried about her, that perhaps she would fare better in an institution where she could be looked after. He sent her away from her daughter for a week when Ava was young.

"You know enough of the world to know that powerful, wealthy men have a way of wielding control over women. Raymond wanted her fortune. Nothing would have stopped him, and in the end, who would the police have believed? Besides, after the fire, it became clear that the danger was only escalating, that if she didn't pretend to be dead, he wouldn't stop until she was.

"When I first came up with this plan, when Elena expressed her desire for vengeance, it wasn't just a matter of making sure Raymond paid for the harm he'd caused, the lives he'd taken. It was our vow that no woman should ever again be abused or murdered at his hand that sustained us."

"Why didn't you tell me earlier? You could have trusted me."

"It wasn't my secret to tell. I promised Elena that I would do everything in my power to help her, that I would keep her existence hidden until it was time to confront Raymond."

"You never intended to marry him."

"No, I didn't."

"And Raymond? Where is he now?"

"I don't know. I wish I did. Elena meant to shoot him, and I was going to help her push the body overboard. We thought if it happened on the last night of the cruise, there was a greater chance he wouldn't be noted as missing by the crew. After all, he had few friends and no family to speak of. But that night—between the weather, the captain's death, and the fire—everything went awry. I've been scouring the lists of survivors and the ones who have been confirmed dead, but it's such a mess. No one knows where anyone is. It will take weeks, maybe months to find out. I was fortunate to have found Ava."

"And Elena?"

Tears fill my eyes. "I don't know. She's not on the list of the deceased, but she's not on the survivor list, either."

She has to be alive. I can't accept that we went through all of this, only for her to lose her life in a fire.

"We always planned to meet after the ship docked, after she killed Raymond. I was going to bring Ava to her so that they could start a new life together in Cuba, under new identities. So tomorrow I'll go like we planned, and all I can do is hope that she will be there. That she will have survived all of this."

"And Ava? What will happen to her if Elena didn't survive?"

He asks the question gently.

"Elena wanted Ava to go to her aunt Marta in Cuba if something happened to her, if the plan failed. Her aunt Marta raised Elena after her parents died, and she promised Elena she would look after Ava. I think it's good for her to be with family. I'm hardly equipped to raise a child. If—" I take a deep breath. "If the worst has happened, then I'll have to take Ava to Cuba to her great-aunt."

"Where will you go?" Harry asks. "Will you stay in New York City?"

"I don't think so. Truthfully, I never liked the city all that much."

"It seems there's a lot I don't know about you."

"True. I suppose we skipped around on some things when we first met. I like green spaces and clean air in my lungs, and I want to live somewhere where I can be happy. Where I can find peace. Where all this ugliness fades away in the background until it is little more than a bad memory. I'd like to see Ireland, where my mother and her parents came from. I don't know where I'll end up just yet, but I think I want to be in the country somewhere."

"You don't think you'll get bored?"

"Maybe. Possibly. After everything, boring doesn't seem so bad."

"It sounds like you have it all figured out, then."

"Not everything," I reply. "Why don't you just come out and ask me what you want to? It's clear you have something on your mind. It's not like you to beat around the bush like this. I thought jewel thieves were supposed to be bold."

"We are. I am. I just—was it real? On the ship? With us?"

"Do you really have to ask after what just happened between us?"

"I think I do."

"Yes. All of it was real. I didn't—I didn't plan on this, on meeting you, on meeting anyone. I wasn't looking to feel this way."

"Me either."

He sounds so disgruntled about it that I can't help but laugh despite the emotions flooding me, because I know how he feels.

This thing between us—love, lust, whatever it is—is damned inconvenient. It's like an itch I can't scratch, the melody to a song that I can't get out of my head, a hunger I can't satiate. All in all, I could live without it entirely, except now he's gotten under my skin like a burr, and I've never been particularly good at denying myself when I wanted something, and it was within my grasp.

He's silent for far longer than I'd like, but then again, I suppose serious decisions like this shouldn't be made with haste even though I'd made mine the second I saw him again.

"That place in the country you mentioned . . . would you be up for a visitor?"

"I suppose it would depend on the visitor," I reply, my heart pounding. "But wouldn't you get bored out there in the country? I imagine it would be quite the change of pace from what you're used to. I doubt there are many diamonds to lift."

"Even novelty gets boring after a while. You aren't the only one who could do with a change of scenery. I've been in this game for a long time now, and while I'm not sure I'll really be out, I wouldn't mind seeing what else is out there. And as to your fears about me being bored, well, I don't think it's possible to be bored in your company."

"You don't know that."

"I have an inkling. Besides, you once asked me when it would be enough, when would I feel like I could cash out. I've made my fortune. Maybe it's time to make something else. I'm wild about you, but then again, you must know that."

I do.

He holds his hand out to me. "Ready for our next adventure, Catherine?"

I smile at him, tears welling in my eyes as I take his outstretched hand.

"If we're going to do this properly, then you should know that my name is Catherine, but I've always preferred to be called Katie."

CHAPTER TWENTY-EIGHT

ELENA

The bar where Miguel works, the location where she and Katie had agreed to meet, is the sort of place that invites regulars and discourages tourists, her impression reinforced by the fact that when she walks in, she's met with a perfunctory nod from the bartender and little else. Three men sit at the bar, but none of them look her way.

Elena glances up at the clock, marking the time. The plan has always been that she and Katie would meet here at noon. She came fifteen minutes early, too nervous to sit in her hotel room, desperate to finally know if Katie and Ava made it out alright. For all that they tried to account for as many possibilities as they could, they never could have predicted the storms, the captain's death, or the fire onboard the *Morro Castle*.

There are times when it feels as though her fear will consume her, the nightmares she experiences now made infinitely worse as she waits for news of Ava, but in her darkest moments, the only thing she has to cling to is her faith: the knowledge that they have survived so many terrible things already; surely, God would not bring them so close to peace and snatch it away so cruelly.

"I'm looking for someone," she tells the bartender.

He doesn't respond.

"His name is Julio. He's Cuban. Like me," she adds for emphasis lest the man think she is here because she works for the government.

There's a beat before the man answers, and her heart pounds, as she waits to hear Julio's fate. She never saw his name on the list of the missing and the deceased, and by all accounts there were people on the boat like the Cubans Julio smuggled out of Havana whose names never showed up on the manifest or any of the official lists. She hasn't been able to help but wonder if, like her, they're out there somewhere, having cast off the remnants of their past lives, free now, or if they lie at the bottom of the sea, bound to be forgotten.

She's wondered more than a time or two whether Julio himself belongs to one of those groups.

She'd looked for him in Asbury Park, but in the aftermath of the fire, there are many unaccounted for, the process of figuring out what happened to all the passengers and crew aboard the *Morro Castle* likely a lengthy one.

"Is he expecting you?" the barman asks her.

She shakes her head, relief flooding her.

So he's alive.

"He'll be happy to see me. You can tell him Elena is here. From the *Morro Castle*."

His eyes widen at the mention of the ship and the tragedy that everyone is now familiar with. The survivors have become famous, their stories printed in newspapers and repeated by many.

"I'll see if he's available," the bartender says before turning his back to her and walking through a door behind the bar.

She sits up on one of the barstools, a fair distance away from the men and their drinks, but it's no matter—even the name of the legendary ship reaching their ears has failed to have any impact. She is anonymous here, and she can instantly see why Julio and Miguel like it and how useful it must be to someone in their line of work.

She looks over at the clock once more. Thirteen minutes until noon.

The door behind the bar opens, and she glances up at the sound, holding her breath as the bartender comes back through, and behind him—

Julio.

She rises from the barstool on shaky legs, reaching out and gripping the edge of the bar before her for purchase.

He stops in the doorway, his gaze settled on her.

"Elena."

He moves forward, wrapping his arms around her and pulling her body toward his.

"Did you jump?" he asks her, his lips inches away from her ear.

"Yes."

"The water—"

"Yes."

There's no need for words between them, no need for elaboration or explanation. As long as she lives, she will never forget what it was like in that water, and she doubts he ever will, either.

"I wasn't sure if you were alive," she says. "I didn't see your name on any of the lists, but with your work, I thought that might be the case, not to mention there's barely any information. I imagine it will be a long time before they're able to account for everyone who was on the ship."

Julio releases her, leading her over to an empty table in the corner, and he asks her all sorts of questions about where she's been and how she's doing. He has the same haunted look in his eyes when he speaks about the *Morro Castle* that she sees when she looks in the mirror, except for her there is the undeniable sense that out of all that horror there has been redemption, too. And finally, the reason she came a little early to see him today—

"On the ship, you told me you procure papers for people. That it is one of the ways you help the Cubans trying to escape."

"I do."

"What happened to them—the family I helped you smuggle out of Havana? Did they survive?"

"They did. Unfortunately, many others did not. Their names will never end up on the official *Morro Castle* rolls."

She swallows past the lump in her throat, the grief for all those lives that were lost, those souls filled with hope as they tried to find freedom.

The clock says it's ten minutes until noon.

"I need your help." Truthfully, she could have asked Miguel for help, and he likely would have given it, but there's also the undeniable fact that she wanted to see Julio again. "The girl I was is officially dead now, and for a whole host of reasons, I have no desire to revive her," Elena continues. "But I realized when I was in the ocean that I'm ready to get on with my life, that I want to *have* a life—a real one. One where I can be free to do as I please. It's a little hard to do that when you're a ghost. I have money for identity documents—Cuban ones, preferably. I can pay you."

He waves her off. "Please. For a friend—it's the least I can do. I can set you up with a new identity if that's what you want."

"It is."

He reaches out and takes her hand, squeezing it gently. "It should take me about a week to get the papers together. Can you come back here?"

She nods, glancing over his shoulder.

Eight minutes to noon.

"Are you living in New York now?" he asks her.

"Temporarily, yes. I have some affairs to finish up here, and then I'd like to return to Cuba."

The desire to go home is overwhelming, the little glimpses she saw during her trip to Havana on the *Morro Castle* leaving her yearning for the country of her birth. She misses her aunt, misses everything, and she longs to raise her daughter in Cuba, to finally bring Ava home.

"We shall see each other, then," he proclaims. "If you'd like, of course. I still have business in Havana, and even though the *Morro Castle* is no more, I will still go home to help when I can."

Seven minutes to noon.

"I would like that very much."

"It's a date," he proposes.

Elena glances over his shoulder. The front door of the bar opens.

She rises from her seat on shaky legs, her gaze locked on the couple entering the bar—Katie and a man—and the little girl between them.

Tears spill down her cheeks, her heart cracking open.

Katie was always punctual.

Their gazes meet across the bar.

There's a silent question in Katie's eyes.

Elena nods.

"Those identity documents," she says, a tremor in her voice, barely able to get the words out past the emotions clogging her throat. "I need a set for me and a set for my daughter."

She moves past him, her future ahead of her, Ava finally returned to her, when Julio calls over his shoulder—

"And your husband? Did he survive?"

EPILOGUE

When he emerges from the water, death's lips pressing a kiss to his spine, the flames burned into his memory, the acrid smell of burning flesh, the tang of salty air in his nostrils, the screams—*God, the screams*—there is one thought running through his mind, one name pushing him forward, his body heaving with the exertion of the swim, his gaze scanning the horizon, the remnants of the ship off somewhere in the distance, the darkness cloaking her bones until all he can see is the fire skating across the ocean.

He falls to his knees, shock slackening his limbs, the weight of his wet evening attire weighing him down like ballast. There's a flurry of movement around him, onlookers coming to the beach, some wading into the water, trying to help, as though there is salvation for all these people, hundreds of souls whose lives have now been relegated to the sea.

The thought is there again, propelling him forward, compelling him to *move*, but no matter how badly he wishes to act, his mind cannot or will not comply, and he lies there crumpled on the sandy shore, her name a croak in his voice, an angry demand for someone to hear him, to render assistance. He tries to reach out to the bodies moving past him, but he can't raise his arms, and despite the dryness in his throat he wants to scream for everyone to listen to him, to tell them that what he has to say is important, that *he* is important.

His head lolls to the side, flashes of images coming back to him—

He struggles to focus now, a sharp stab of fear spreading throughout his chest.

The fire.

God, he remembers the fire.

"Were you on the ship?" a voice demands, urgently now, and he blinks, tearing his gaze from the blood-soaked sand beside him.

He can't feel anything, whatever pain his injury might have caused lanced by the brutal numbness of the hell he just escaped.

"You're injured," the voice says—a man's voice by the sound of it, and it takes all his energy to turn toward the voice, to stare up at the body looming over him.

"H—help—" The words stick in his throat. "Wa—water—"

The man leans down closer to him, and then the shouting around him grows louder, a pounding noise in his brain, and he wants to scream at them to shut up, but the rush of anger passes as quickly as it came, and then he feels as though he is falling, falling into the sand, his body sinking away from him, and for one horrible wretched moment, he imagines he is in the water again, in that moment when he decided he must live, when the inky black surrounded him and he was irrevocably alone in the abyss.

And then, once more, the darkness overtakes him.

When he wakes, he has no idea if he's been out for hours or days, only that the sun is shining through a window, the brightness overwhelming in its intensity. He no longer lies on a bed of sand, but scratchy, bright white sheets.

Her name is on his lips once more.

The woman he killed.

His wife.

A flurry of activity surrounds him, the air filled with a faint, antiseptic bite and he realizes he is lying in a hospital bed, although where the ship ended up when it caught fire is beyond him. They were near the end of the cruise—they must be somewhere close to New York now.

But where?

Where is she?

A nurse rushes past him, and he calls out to her, but his voice is little more than a whisper.

She continues without a second glance, rage filling him, and then, finally, a different nurse stops in front of him.

"You're awake. Good. We've been worried about you," she says, her voice injected with a briskness that some part of him is relieved to hear, the impression that she isn't maudlin or rattled giving him a greater confidence in her efficiency in the whole business.

For a man used to maneuvering his own fortunes, finding himself in the charge of another is a difficult circumstance to acclimate to and reconcile.

"There was a woman," he tries again, his voice more confident now, sure, the croak he heard before a sliver of panic that is now abated by the sight of the nurse. He must get this right. She must hear him. *No, that's not right,* he corrects himself. For a moment, he can't form the words, seized by some memory he simply cannot untangle, the drugs they've given him mixing with the alcohol he now remembers drinking earlier, long before everything went amiss. "There are two women. What can you tell me about them? Are they here?"

The nurse bustles past him, checking a chart perched somewhere outside his view, stretched above him too high to be of any use to him now. He can't remember the last time he felt so helpless, resigned to such a state of unimportance. Childhood, perhaps, but even then—

No—

He can't remember ever feeling this way.

Their names are on his lips, but as soon as he tries to say them it feels as though the words slip down his throat like sands through an hourglass.

"You've had a shock," the nurse says, leaning down and laying her hand on his chest. Only then does he realize how much he has been squirming in his hospital bed, how desperate he has been to move. "You were injured when the ship went down, and—"

"—The ship. The *Morro Castle*. How bad is it? What happened to her?" he demands.

He's caught off guard by how drained those few questions leave him, how much effort it takes to elicit such small pieces of information.

"It was a terrible thing," the nurse whispers, and then she makes the sign of the cross over herself. "Those poor souls."

He can feel it overtaking him again, the darkness, the sleep, the weight of his body pulling him down into the depths of the deep blue sea once more. He grips the crisp white hospital sheets with his fingers, holding on for something to tether him to the here and now, to chase the nightmares away.

The nurse shouts for a doctor to help, but she sounds so very far away, and he is convinced that he is in the great, heaving depths of the ocean once more and it is pulling him under.

He can barely make out fragments of the conversation . . . their voices growing fainter and fainter . . .

"Terrible thing he's been through . . . the fire . . . for the ship to go down like that . . . besides, he's been shot."

When he wakes, his whole-body aches, the pain nearly unbearable. The tent has gotten more crowded since the morning, the other survivors taking up space beside him.

The pain feels like nothing he has ever experienced before, and suddenly, he knows with a certain dread, that he is dying.

A nurse walks over to him.

"Mr. Warner? Your wife is here."

He opens his mouth to tell her he doesn't want to see anyone, that he isn't feeling well, that he needs more pain medicine. Can't she see he's dying? But before he can speak, she's already walking away, and another woman walks toward him.

Her face haunts his nightmares now.

Elena stands beside his bed, dressed in a pale blue gown.

She is vengeance.

He feels like he's floating, drifting away, and the last thing he sees before the life fades from his body is her face.

His last heiress.

The Cuban heiress.

AUTHOR'S NOTE

On September 8, 1934, the SS *Morro Castle* caught fire on the way from Havana to New York City. The fire broke out in the early-morning hours while many passengers were enjoying a last night of festivities aboard the luxurious vessel that sailed on a weeklong cruise from New York to Havana. The fire wasn't the only thing that was auspicious about that night—hours earlier, the ship's captain died under mysterious circumstances, leaving the crew in a state of panic, particularly because the weather conditions were deteriorating at the time as the *Morro Castle* was caught between two storms—a nor'easter and the edge of a hurricane.

Eventually, the ship ended up beached on the New Jersey shoreline near Asbury Park, where tourists flocked to the scene to see the legendary cruise ship and locals gave aid to the survivors. Officially, 137 of the 549 passengers and crew onboard the *Morro Castle* were reported as deceased—most of them passengers on the ship. Because there were reportedly individuals who were unaccounted for on the manifest, it's likely that the death toll was higher.

Prior to that fateful night in 1934, the *Morro Castle* had a notorious history. During Prohibition, it provided a week of indulgence for its guests who were able to partake in drinking and partying onboard. It was also rumored that arms and people were being transported on the ship given the political tensions in Cuba at the time. There were further rumors of discontent among the crew, and the captain himself expressed concerns of a mutiny and fears that someone was trying to poison him onboard the ship prior to his death.

While the cause of the fire has never been officially settled and there are still questions about the captain's death, official and unofficial investigations surrounding the fire's origins have led to numerous theories, including arson, sabotage, insurance fraud, design flaws, negligence, and more. Much of that fateful final night aboard the *Morro Castle* is shrouded in mystery, but the legacy of the ship's tragedy has led to an increase in safety standards for modern cruise ships.

If you're interested in learning more about the *Morro Castle*, the following nonfiction books cover the ship and its history:

The Morro Castle: *Tragedy at Sea*, by Hal Burton
Inferno at Sea: Stories of Death and Survival Aboard the
    Morro Castle, by Gretchen F. Coyle and Deborah C.
    Whitcraft

Fire at Sea: The Mysterious Tragedy of the Morro Castle, by
    Thomas Gallagher

When the Dancing Stopped: The Real Story of the Morro
    Castle *Disaster and its Deadly Wake*, by Brian Hicks

Shipwreck: The Strange Fate of the Morro Castle, by Gordon
    Thomas and Max Morgan-Witts

As an author, curiosity often shapes the subjects that I choose to write about. I spend so much time researching, writing, and speaking about my novels that it's always important to me that I'm passionate about—and fascinated by—the topics that I explore. I first learned about the *Morro Castle* a few years ago, and I was moved by the drama and tragedy of the ship's final voyage. I started to think about the fictional characters that would inhabit the story, why they would find themselves on the ship, and how the journey would impact their lives.

From this curiosity, Catherine and Elena were born. I was instantly drawn to their friendship, loyalty, and their passion for seeing justice served. I was also inspired by the courageous actions of so many onboard the *Morro Castle*, as well as the mystery surrounding the ship's final voyage.

Thank you so much for reading *The Cuban Heiress*.

ACKNOWLEDGMENTS

If there's one thing that's consistent in my writing process, it's that the magic happens after I turn the book in to my editor. For nine years now, we've worked together on twelve novels, and I am so grateful to Kate Seaver for her guidance, patience (especially on those tough edit rounds), and editorial insights. The relationship between author and editor is so key to a book's development, and I am incredibly fortunate to have a creative partner that I wholly trust and who is such a fierce champion of me and my books.

Thank you to my extraordinary agent Kevan Lyon, who has been guiding my career for eleven years. I can't imagine where I'd be without Kevan's hard work, passion, professionalism, and dedication. I couldn't ask for a better advocate to have in my corner.

Thank you so much to all the readers who have taken a chance on my books. I am so grateful for the love and enthusiasm you've shown my characters. Thank you to the amazing community of booklovers at Reese's Book Club.

ACKNOWLEDGMENTS

My wonderful publicists Tara O'Connor and Stephanie Felty and marketing representatives Fareeda Bullert, Jessica Mangicaro, and Hillary Tacuri work so hard to get my books out into the world and into readers' hands. Thank you for all your tremendous efforts on my behalf. I'm so fortunate to work with such a fabulous team of creative professionals.

Penguin Random House and Berkley have provided such a supportive home for me and my books. Thank you to Madeline McIntosh, Allison Dobson, Ivan Held, Christine Ball, Claire Zion, Jeanne-Marie Hudson, Craig Burke, Erin Galloway, Tawanna Sullivan, and Amanda Maurer for all you do. Thank you as well to the sales and subrights departments, as well as the art department who creates my gorgeous covers.

I'm so grateful for my friends and colleagues for your encouragement. It means a great deal to work alongside such wonderful people whose talents constantly inspire me.

Thank you to my family whose love and support means everything. Every book I write is for you.

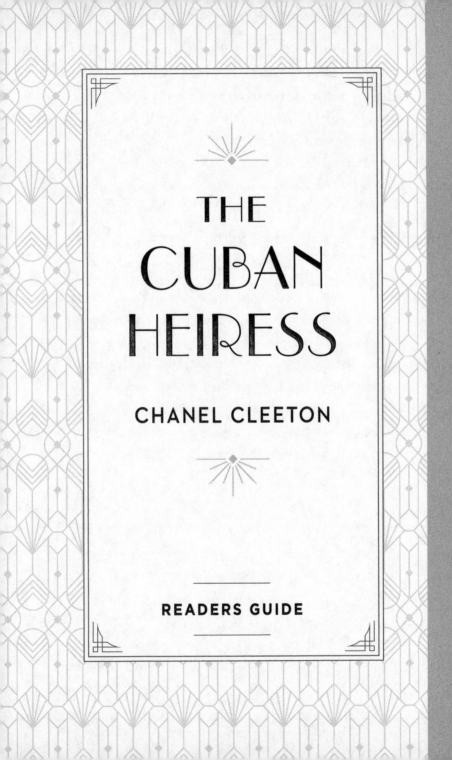

THE
CUBAN
HEIRESS

CHANEL CLEETON

QUESTIONS FOR DISCUSSION

1. Which heroine did you identify with more—Elena or Catherine? What characteristics in their personalities did you find similarities with? What differences?

2. Many of the characters throughout the novel make sacrifices on behalf of others. What examples did you find? Did you agree with the characters' actions in these situations? How would you have handled these decisions?

3. In this story, the *Morro Castle* sets sail in 1934, during the Great Depression and a year after the Cuban Revolution of 1933. How do these two events affect the characters, the setting, and the story?

4. Both Catherine and Harry board the *Morro Castle* with their own agendas and as outsiders on the ship. How do they relate to each other? How does this bring them closer throughout the cruise?

5. Catherine and Harry are both faced with difficult decisions in their lives where they are confronted with an opportunity to avenge people who were wronged by another. Do you see similarities in their situations? Do you agree with how they handled these decisions? Why or why not?

6. What role does motherhood play in the choices Elena makes throughout the novel? What sacrifices does she make for her daughter? How does her love for Ava motivate her?

7. Throughout the cruise, a friendship develops between Elena and Julio. What experiences bring them together? What do they have in common? Do you think their friendship will blossom into something more?

8. Elena and Catherine are both heavily influenced by the trauma they have experienced—first the fire in New York City, and then the fire onboard the *Morro Castle*. How do they both handle what they've experienced? How does it define them? How do they use it to further their aims?

9. Have you ever traveled on a cruise ship? What was your experience like?

10. Prior to reading *The Cuban Heiress*, were you familiar with the *Morro Castle*? Were you surprised by what you learned

about the ship? What do you think caused the fire on-board?

11. At the time, the *Morro Castle* fire drew a great deal of attention and had a huge impact on those who survived the fire as well as the rest of the world. How do you think the fire shaped the characters' lives? What similar world events have influenced your life? What memories do you have of them?

CHANEL CLEETON is the *New York Times* and *USA Today* bestselling author of *The Most Beautiful Girl in Cuba*, *The Last Train to Key West*, *When We Left Cuba*, *Our Last Days in Barcelona*, and Reese's Book Club pick *Next Year in Havana*. Originally from Florida, she grew up on stories of her family's exodus from Cuba following the events of the Cuban Revolution. Her passion for politics and history continued during her years spent studying in England, where she earned a bachelor's degree in international relations from Richmond, the American International University in London, and a master's degree in global politics from the London School of Economics and Political Science. Cleeton also received her Juris Doctor from the University of South Carolina School of Law.

Ready to find
your next great read?

Let us help.

Visit prh.com/nextread

Penguin
Random
House